The Yearning Heart

The Yearning Heart

A Sequel to **BANNER OF LOVE**

By

Joyce Haskell Frost

"Understanding is a wellspring of life unto him that hath it."
Proverbs 16:22A

Wellspring Books
Route 1, Box 27
Groton, Vermont   05046

Bible verses from King James Version

All characters and incidents in this book are fictitious, and any resemblance to actual persons or incidents is purely coincidental.

Copyright © 1990 by Joyce Haskell Frost

Edited by Carol Arnson
Cover Design & Illustrations by Stephanie Gordon
Typeset by Marilyn Gomrick

All rights reserved. No part of this book may be reproduced or transmitted in any form or by any means, electonic or mechanical, including photocopying, recording, or by any information storage and retrieval system, without permission in writing from the publisher.

ISBN 0-9614712-6-3

PRINTED IN THE UNITED STATES OF AMERICA

DEDICATED

to the

GLORY

of

GOD

"And God said, Let us make man in our image, after our likeness . . . So God created man in his own image, in the image of God created he him; male and female created he them."

Genesis 1:26a - Genesis 1:27

CAST OF CHARACTERS

LYDIA ROBERTS: Widow and manager of the Roberts family Vermont-based all-season resort.

ANDREW ROBERTS: Lydia's father-in-law who joined the family shortly after his only son died. Known as 'Gramps' by family and friends, he is the spiritual giant of the Roberts clan.

ANDREA (Lydia's daughter) AND GREG HOLLOWAY: Jason, 16 (Andrea's son and Greg's adopted son); their children, Andrew Roberts (Robbie), 10; Sara, age 5 and Rebecca (Becky), 3-1/2.

JEFFERY ROBERTS (Lydia's son) AND HIS WIFE, SYLVIA: Their three children: Anne, 12; Jeffery III, 9; Lydia Jane (Jane), nearly 4.

ALEXANDER HARRISON: Jason's grandfather, now affectionately known as Grand; his wife, Ellyn (Greg's cousin); and their four-year-old son, Nathan.

REGINALD THOMAS: A charming, somewhat colorful bachelor, state senator, real estate and insurance salesman; also a friend of the Roberts family.

SUSAN (Greg's sister) AND JOHN THORPE: Their three children: Jerry, 17; Mike, 15; and Julie, 8.

CORY AND JANELLE PHILLIPS: Their three children: Richard (Ricky), 9; Tricia, 7-1/2; and Beatrice (Bede), nearly 4.

GRETCHEN NELSON: 17. Pianist at The Farm chapel.

MATT ANDERSON: Resort maintenance man, and his wife, Kate, housekeeping supervisor.

CYNTHIA MARSH: Matt's niece - a new employee at The Farm.

KEN ROSS: Summer chaplain at The Farm and a protege of Alex Harrison's.

Plus—several other characters you'll rediscover or meet anew as the story unfolds.

CHRISTIAN NOVELS BY JOYCE HASKELL FROST

Contemporary titles

'ANDREA' series

- THE HEART OF ANDREA
- FOLLOW YOUR HEART
- BANNER OF LOVE
- THE YEARNING HEART

'JENNIE' series

- JENNIE'S PATHWAY
- JENNIE'S PARSONAGE LIFE

Turn-of-the-Century Novel

- LOVE WAS WAITING

If not available at your local bookstore, contact WELLSPRING BOOKS for information.

THE YEARNING HEART

CHAPTER ONE

The ending of a perfect June day in Vermont closed in on the Holloway patio. Andrea's gaze rested on the lush green of the heavily-leaved trees which covered the mountain that sloped steadily upward a short distance behind The Farm, the Roberts' family resort. She murmured under her breath, "What is so rare as a day in June?" forgetting for the moment who penned the words.

Her thoughts were brought sharply back to the family members who had been invited to the Holloways to celebrate the return of Lydia Roberts and Gramps from a much-needed vacation. Lydia seemed to be in high gear as she spoke to her grandson. "Would you like to come to the office Monday morning, Jason, to go over the reservations and then take first shift at the desk?"

"Sure thing, Nan," Jason enthused. He no longer called his grandmother Nana but shortened it to Nan, to which she had no objections.

Andrea's eyes rested for a moment on her

oldest son, over six feet tall, already handsome with his shock of wheat-colored hair and deep-set blue eyes. Sixteen already! For the past two years he had been consistently declaring that his goal in life was to help manage The Farm and now it appeared his grandmother was going to give him an opportunity to convince them all that he was serious. His mother felt as pleased as Jason was. It would be wonderful to have him settle close by and take an interest in the family business.

Her attention shifted to her mother as she was saying above the prattle of voices, the children's shouts and the usual hub-bub that accompanied their family gatherings, "Listen, everyone, we have an important decision to make. Matt came to me early this morning with a request that I feel we should honor; the Andersons have been so loyal to us over the years."

"Well, what is it?" Jeff asked. "Is it something we can do without putting an extra burden on you, Mother?" Jeff Roberts was also fond of the Andersons who had come to The Farm to work while Jeff, Senior was still alive, Matt as maintenance man and his wife Kate as director of housekeeping.

"It would be a help to me," Lydia responded. "It's like this," she continued. "Matt's niece, Cynthia Marsh, would like to come to The Farm to work for a time. She feels the need to get away from home. It seems that the man she was going to marry left her practically at the altar to run away with a so-called friend of hers. She feels humiliated in the presence of their friends. Remember when Matt and Kate came to Christ a few years ago? Matt then tried to make up with his only sister with whom he had quarreled in his younger years and hadn't seen since. She rejected his overtures and would barely speak to him or Kate when they went to see them but Cynthia, their daughter, was intrigued by her new-found uncle and has kept in touch with him ever since."

"Wasn't she the one who visited the Andersons for a few days after she graduated from high school?" Sylvia, Jeff's wife, asked.

"Yes, that was Cynthia. She called Matt last evening. She's dreadfully upset right now and Matt feels we could help her spiritually. She has been mixed up in some new cult for about two years and Matt is very concerned about her. He feels right now that she needs a stabilizing influence in her life and that we might be able to help."

"Do it then, Mom," Andrea encouraged. Andrea and her brother Jeff were co-owners of The Farm with their mother Lydia. She valued their opinions as she did her elderly father-in-law who made his home with them, helping out nearly everywhere.

"What do you think, Gramps?" Lydia asked Andrew Roberts, who was affectionately known to everyone as 'Gramps'.

"It does seem as though God has given us the privilege of helping those with spiritual needs. I agree that if it wouldn't be extra work for you it would be the thing to do," Gramps answered.

"I say let her come," Jason remarked. "Maybe she can find a man here."

This remark brought a shout of laughter from the family.

"Well," Jason said defensively, "Dad met Mom here, Jim and Myrna met here, Janelle found Cory, Lisa and Kurt got together here, and what about Cousin Ellyn and my grandfather, Alex. Right?"

"Right," answered his grandmother, "but we are **not** running a matchmaking service, Jason."

"I believe God works out those details," Gramps said gently, "if we do our part in reaching out to those in need and present a living testimony of Jesus Christ to them. Lydia, the thing is, what would she be doing? I believe everyone should have a meaningful job to do."

"That's no problem," Lydia quickly answered. "She has had both training and experience in hotel management. She could be my assistant. It would be an answer to a prayer for me."

"But I thought I was going to help, Nan. Would she take my place?" Jason asked anxiously.

"No, of course not, Jason, she would no doubt be of great help to you, too."

"By all means let's welcome her," Jeff said, "if it will help you in any way, Mother, I'm all for it."

"It appears to me that you all might need each other," Greg said. Andrea cast a loving look his way. This remark sounded so typical of her husband, always ready to reach out to someone in need.

"Shouldn't Grand be in on this?" Jason inquired. Jason's grandfather, Alex Harrison, had bought an interest in the resort and put up the funds for the chapel and now the new dorm. Both of these extended the gospel outreach for which The Farm had gradually become known during the past five years.

"He never has wanted to be bothered with the everyday problems that confront us. I don't see how this would make any difference to him. As long as **you** are all in agreement, I'll call it settled." Lydia continued, "I'll have Matt call Cynthia and tell her to come as soon as she can."

"By the way, Mother," Greg asked, "when is Ken Ross due to arrive?"

"Tomorrow," Lydia replied. "I'm so happy he's returning this year. I felt he was just the young man we needed for the chapel and the guests liked him so much, as I'm sure you all noticed."

"I sure did," Jason spoke up. "He'll be great for the teen weeks we've planned, Nan. I'm really looking forward to staying in the new dorm with all the guys. I'll be glad when Jerry gets here. I can't wait to see him."

Jerry Thorp, Jason's cousin, had been Ken Ross's assistant with sports the preceding year and was returning to help in that capacity once again.

"Shouldn't the Thorps be here soon, Dad?"

Jason asked.

"Anytime, son," Greg answered.

In the meantime, Sara, Greg and Andrea's five-year-old daughter, had crawled onto her daddy's lap, while their youngest daughter, Becky, who was three and a half, edged closer to Jason who had pulled her onto his knees and was cuddling her. Becky was his favorite although he tried not to show it.

Andrea eyed them lovingly. Jason had so many facets in his makeup that one never knew how he would respond in any given situation, but she breathed a quick prayer of thanks that he appeared to be outgrowing most of them.

After a brief discussion concerning The Farm and its many ramifications, Lydia and Gramps left, followed shortly by Jeff and his family.

Thanks for a nice day, Sis," Jeff said to Andrea. "We are surely blessed with a beautiful family, aren't we?"

"Sure are, Jeff. I do pray it will work out with Cynthia. I wouldn't want her bringing any false beliefs that she might have into our family circle or to The Farm."

"I think we can trust Gramps to curtail any of that, along with Ken's help. A matter for prayer, Sis. 'Night, Greg. See you at church."

"Come on, girls, bath time and bed for you."

"Daddy will read us a story first, won't he?" Sara demanded.

"Yes, a story, Daddy," Becky echoed.

"Of course, darlings. I'll be in soon," Greg answered. "We'll have our Bible story and prayer time."

Just as the girls were ready to hop into bed, Robbie called, "Here they come. Here's Jerry and Mike."

"And Julie?" called Sara. "I want to see Julie."

Andrea sighed. She did like to get the children in bed early on a Saturday night but this was a special occasion and Julie did love her cousins very much.

It was a hub-bub as the families greeted each other, all trying to talk at the same time. Julie made a beeline for the girls' room which delighted Sara and Becky. It took awhile to get the girls all settled down as Julie had a cot in the girls' room, but it was finally accomplished.

Mike went to Robbie's room with him, while the rest of them lingered in the living room awhile, enjoying the peacefulness.

"How long can you stay, Sue?" Andrea inquired.

"At least until Jerry is settled. We have a few days. When are you moving into the dorm, Jason?" Sue asked her nephew.

"Early Monday morning," Jason answered quickly. It had been a hassle to get his parents to agree to his staying there all summer instead of just when he was needed for counseling.

"You finished your course in personal evangelism Ken sent you, Jere?" Jason asked his cousin.

"Yup. You?"

"Sure did."

"It should be a help this summer. I felt like a dud last year. Although Ken was swell and Gramps—well, you can't beat Gramps with the boys—all the kids like him—as a matter of fact—all the guests of all ages like Gramps . . ."

"No one like my Gramps," Jason replied, "unless it's my Dad."

Andrea's eyes showed her pleasure at that remark. Basically Jason loved Greg, but as his adopted son had, at times, shown signs of rebellion which, she thanked God, he was rapidly outgrowing. In fact, he and Greg had a very sound relationship now, as good as their ten-year-old son, Robbie.

Jerry asked, trying to be casual, "Is Gretchen Nelson going to be on staff again this summer?"

"Yup. She's going to be the pianist again."

A pleased look crossed Jerry's face and a momentary jealous one was on Jason's. Why did Jerry have to get mixed up with girls anyway!

14

"You still like her?" he asked.

"Yeah," Jerry responded, still trying to be casual. "She's okay."

"Only okay?" Jason asked a bit sarcastically.

"Well, she's pretty with her light blonde hair and those startling blue eyes with the dark lashes."

"Oh—oh—you got it bad, boy."

"Well—maybe . . ." Jerry laughed a bit self-consciously.

Greg broke in, "Time you guys hit the sack, isn't it?" He yawned. "Excuse me, folks, but it's time for me, also. Sunday school and church tomorrow, you know, but let's have a circle of prayer first, committing the boys and their service for the Lord this summer into His hands."

CHAPTER TWO

Alex Harrison and his wife Ellyn, who was also Sue's cousin, with their four-year-old son, Nathan, had been invited for the Sunday noon meal at the Holloways to give the cousins an opportunity to chat and the kids to get better acquainted. Nathan had been such a delightful surprise for Alex and Ellyn. As Ellyn often remarked, he and Alex made up for all the misery she had suffered in her first marriage, from which she had been released by her husband's death.

Nathan looked so much like Jason, who had made a big deal about calling him Uncle.

Andrea woke early Sunday morning. It was too early to get up and as she lay there thinking about Alex, Ellyn and Nathan coming to dinner, her thoughts drifted back to the year Nathan was born. Jason was twelve then. He was quite jealous of Nathan as he had had his grandfather, Alex's, attention so completely. Alex had not changed one iota toward Jason, but Jason had suddenly begun asking questions and demanding answers about his own father, Alex's son Peter, who had died in a snowmobile accident. This was a time Andrea had dreaded—Jason would have to know that his mother had not been married to his father. But Greg, bless him, came up with an idea ... she remembered as though it were yesterday.

"Andrea, why don't I go on the Canadian fishing trip with Gramps, Alex and Jason this year? Between us, we'll think of a way to answer all of Jason's questions about his father."

"But you don't like to fish, Greg."

"Does that matter? We need to get this behind us. Jason is becoming difficult to handle. I think he should know the whole story."

"All right, Greg, and thank you so much. I love you so, darling, you are such a good father to my son, as though he were your own."

"I love him like a son. I never think of him in any other way," he answered simply.

"I know, dear, and I appreciate that."

"So I'll tell Jason that I'll be going along this year."

When Jason was told, he only shrugged and said, "Okay by me."

Greg never did tell Andrea all that happened but she had pieced together what she had been told by all four of them, to get Jason to accept the truth about his own father, and she guessed that it had been a rugged time.

Jason became very subdued and quiet but treated his mother the same as always. Then one day he approached her soon after Becky was born and said, "It's okay, Mom. I love you and Dad. I appreciate him now and I don't ever want to be the kind of man my own father was. He broke Grand's heart but Grand feels he was mostly to blame. I understand now why I have to be dealt with when I display my temper." Giving her a tight squeeze and a kiss on the cheek, he said, "Thanks for marrying Dad, Mom, he's a good father to me."

The subject was never mentioned again, but once in awhile Jason would be more affectionate than at other times and say something like, "We have a nice family, Mom, don't we?"

Brushing away a tear, she sent a prayer of gratitude to her Heavenly Father for His merciful goodness to her. And prayed for His continued guidance in their lives.

Glancing at the clock, she decided it was time to get the household moving if they were to get to church on time.

* * * * *

That afternoon the Holloways and their guests were lounging on the patio, enjoying a time of leisure following a picnic meal.

"Listen to Julie, will you?" Sue said. They were all quiet for a few minutes listening to Julie talk to the smaller children. She had Sara, Becky, Nathan and an array of the girls' dolls all lined up on the grass as she went through the motions of a Sunday school teacher.

"Sara, pay attention now, and Nathan, stop wiggling. Why can't you be as good as Becky and the others?" indicating the row of dolls and ignoring the fact that Becky was nearly asleep . . .

"I wanna play in the sandbox," Nathan declared.

Andrea murmured, "I'd better put Becky in for a nap, she's nearly asleep now."

"Let me take her in," Greg offered. "You sit still, hon."

"Okay. It is comfy here and I feel lazy. Better put a light blanket over her."

"Will do," Greg replied, planting a kiss on her cheek as she smiled sleepily at him.

"Time to let your class go, Julie," her mother said. At these words, Nathan bounded toward the sandbox and was soon engrossed in the mechanism of Robbie's old toys which miraculously still worked.

"But what can I do?" Julie asked.

"Didn't you bring along some of your favorite books?" her father asked.

Her face brightened as she trotted toward the house. "Yeah. I forgot."

"Sara, hadn't you better have a nap, too?" Andrea asked.

But Sara shook her head and said, "I'll just sit on your lap, Mom."

"The boys are taking a long walk, aren't they?" Greg inquired as he returned.

Alex spoke up. "I heard Jason say that after today the place would be overrun with guests, so this was the only really free time they had to walk over the grounds."

Around four o'clock Ken Ross appeared around the corner of the house. "Hello there, everyone."

Alex was on his feet immediately, moving quickly toward the very blonde young man of whom one of the girls last year had said, "Wow, he looks like the typical all-American football hero." As, indeed, he did, with his broad shoulders and slim hips.

"Hi there, boy," Alex said as he grasped Ken's hand and placed his other arm across his shoulders. "How goes it?"

Ken grinned. "Great. Graduation went well. Now I'm ready for work."

After being warmly greeted by everyone and having been offered something to eat by Andrea, which he refused saying he had stopped for a meal only a short time ago, Ken said, "Guess I'd better report to Mrs. Roberts and then unload my stuff."

"I'll go with you. Got some things to talk about. You want to wait here, Ellyn?" he asked his wife.

"No, I think I'll take Nathan home. He needs a bath by the looks of him, and then I'll see if he'll settle for a nap to get ready for church tonight."

"Okay, see you at the house later then." Turning to Greg and John he asked, "You fellows want to come along?"

"Might as well," Greg answered.

"Where is Jason?" Ken inquired, "and Jerry?"

"They went for a walk. It's time they were coming back. We'll probably run into them somewhere on the grounds."

As the men walked to Ken's car, he inquired of Alex, "Did you get the swimming pool in yet?"

"Just finished this week," Alex assured him. It had been decided that an Olympic-sized swimming pool was needed for the teen weeks, so had been a last-minute project.

Ken drove his car directly to the dorm and left it while he went to see Lydia. The other men reached there about the same time. By helping, they made short work of unloading all of his gear. "Boy, it seems good to be back."

Just then all four boys burst into the dorm, greeting Ken enthusiastically. "We'll be moving in tomorrow, Ken," Jason informed him.

"Great. We'll have plenty to do. Alex, we'll need to have a meeting to discuss details. Mrs. Roberts says that this is your business, same as last year."

"Okay, why don't you come to my house for breakfast after which we'll go over the program."

"Sounds good. I'll be there," Ken assured him.

"Right now we need to go home and get ready for church," Greg said. "Come on, you guys. Will we see you there, Ken?"

"Wouldn't miss it. I always like to hear your pastor. I'll have plenty of time to listen to myself the rest of the summer!"

"See ya in the morning, Ken. We will probably be settled in by the time you get back from Grand's house," Jason said.

"We have only a dozen or so teen boys this week, so that will give us a good chance to get into the swing of things. Perhaps we can arrange a few activities for the girls, too.

—

* * * * *

The following morning was hectic in the Holloway home. Between getting Greg off to work, gathering together last-minute things for Jason, and trying to be friendly with their house guests, Andrea was an extremely busy person. It helped when Julie offered to dress Becky and help with her breakfast. Becky rebelled at first at the table because Jason always sat by her and helped her. She couldn't quite understand that he would be away at meal time for several weeks.

"Listen, Becky, I'll be at The Farm, but I promise to drop by and see you sometime each day if possible, okay?"

"Okay," Becky said with a bewildered look.

"Me, too, Jason?" Sara demanded.

"Of course, you, too," he assured her.

"In the meantime, why can't I help Becky?" Robbie asked.

"That would be wonderful, Robbie." Andrea gave her ten-year-old son an appreciative look. She knew he often felt left out. "Okay with you, Becky?"

"Okay," Becky smiled, but with a somewhat doubtful look.

When the boys were ready to leave, accompanied by Jerry's dad, his mother offered to go with them but Jerry protested, "Mom!" And she backed away.

Jason noticed the wistful look on Andrea's face and said, "Mom, I'm not going to the end of the world. You'll see me every day, I promise. Especially," he laughed, "when I bring you my laundry bag."

"Oh, go on with you! I've got work to do," she smiled as a tear dropped unheeded onto her cheek.

With them out of the way and Robbie off to The Farm where he did occasional chores that a boy of his age could do, and the three girls playing outside, the sisters-in-law settled down for a cup

21

of coffee.

"Life brings changes, Sue," Andrea said.

"Indeed it does. But you'll have Jason close by. We have to let go sometimes, Andrea. If we have instilled strong Christian standards in them, and I believe we've tried to do just that, then it's time for them to be tested. Not that they will meet with much of it right here. But they will have Ken and Gramps and Greg, if necessary."

"You're so right, Sue." Changing the subject she remarked, "We'll have an easy day as Ellyn invited us all to dinner tonight. My, it seems so good to see Ellyn blossom in her new happiness, doesn't it?"

"Sure does. And she's not a bit different with all the wealth at her disposal."

"I'd be so intimidated by a live-in housekeeper and maid," Andrea said.

"So would I," Sue agreed, "but Ellyn seems to take it in stride. She always says that she is so thankful to you and Greg for taking her in, in her time of need, and for helping restore her faith in God."

"And to think she almost missed this happiness thinking she wasn't good enough for Alex."

"Time has proven her to be so wrong on that score. I'm looking forward to this afternoon. Remember she invited us and the kids over early?"

"Yes, I thought we could go around three. Becky should be up from her nap by then. I'd better get busy with the housework."

"Okay, and I'm going to help." The sisters-in-law worked swiftly and in harmony all morning.

"I'm going to bake a batch of chocolate chip cookies for the boys to take to the dorm for snacks, and while I'm at it, I'll make some with M&Ms for the kids here."

"Okay, I'll go out with the girls," Sue answered.

When Andrea gave Jason the bag of cookies later that day he said, "Thanks loads, Mom. They'll sure taste good." Then he gave her one of his special embraces that were scarce but precious as he drew her into his arms with a tight squeeze and kissed her lightly on the cheek several times, whispering in her ear, "I love you, Mom. You're really special to me."

"Thank you, son." Then to cover up her emotions she said, "I expect you to behave yourself this summer!"

Grinning, he retorted, "Don't I always?"

She watched him from the doorway as he lifted Becky up, kissed her and went off whistling.

CHAPTER THREE

As Andrea drove her car into the Harrison driveway that afternoon, Sue said, "Aren't you glad Alex and Ellyn decided to live here?"

"Oh, yes. I was surprised, though, when Alex sold his New Haven home and bought this lot from us to build a house on. Really, Sue, wouldn't you call it a small mansion?"

"Yes, but Ellyn has made it homey."

"Just look at these grounds! Aren't they gorgeous! And the way Alex had the brush all cleared out so you can get glimpses of the house from the road and on this winding drive."

"It's indeed lovely," Sue answered.

Ellyn was waiting at the front door for them. "Hi. Come right in. Nathan is out in his play yard if the girls want to join him. Sara knows the way, don't you, Sara?"

Sara looked at her mother expectantly. "It's okay, dear." At this, Sara led the way through the house to the back yard.

Ellyn took her guests down the expansive hallway past the drawing room and front parlor and the other rooms to the den, of which she said, "This is my favorite room. This is where we really live. Make yourselves at home. I'll just take a minute to see if the kids are okay." She was back directly. "Sometimes Nathan gets very possessive with his things but he seems to be sharing with the girls today."

"No doubt Julie will boss them around some," Sue said dryly.

"My girls will love it," Andrea declared.

"How would it be if we feed the children around five or so, then the maid can watch them while we enjoy our dinner?"

"Sounds like a lovely idea to me," Andrea replied.

"Same here," Sue agreed.

"How are Uncle Doug and Aunt Irene?" Ellyn inquired.

"Fine," Sue answered. "They are coming up soon for a week with Greg and his family and by the end of August we'll all be here until Jerry is ready to leave."

"And you and your family will stay here with us, right?" Ellyn asked.

"If you are sure you still want us, we'd love it. It would leave more comfortable space for Mom and Dad at Greg's."

"What about Mike?" Andrea asked. "I thought he would be staying with us. I do hope so as Robbie will be so disappointed if he doesn't."

"I do think he wants to stay with Robbie," Sue assured her.

"And Julie?" Andrea asked.

"She can spend as much time with the girls as she wants, but I'd like her with me nights."

"Alex is going to New Haven for a few days next week. He's going to leave Nathan and me at White Plains and pick us up on his way back. It makes a longer trip to go that way but the folks haven't seen Nathan in a while and Dad is crazy about him." Ellyn had been on the outs with her parents for a time, but since her marriage to Alex and especially since Nathan's birth the breach had been healed.

"Will you see my folks?" Sue asked.

"I surely will. I'll never cease to be grateful for all the help they gave me when Melvin died, and after."

The afternoon passed quickly and pleasantly until it was time for the children to eat. When Julie learned they were to eat earlier than the adults, she begged to join them saying, "Then I can help watch them while you eat dinner also, Mom."

"That sounds like a good idea, sweetie," Sue answered.

Just as the children finished eating, Alex arrived. Nathan rushed to greet his father, with the girls at his heels calling, "Hi, Grandpa Alex."

Alex played with them for a few minutes before he said, "I'd better shower and shave before the rest of our guests arrive."

Nathan teased to go back outside to play, telling his mother, "We have to finish making our castle."

"Okay, for an hour or so, but you come in directly when you are called."

"Okay, Mom, come on, girls," he shouted heading for the door.

"What a bundle of energy they all are," Andrea laughed.

Greg, John, Robbie and Mike arrived just as Alex reappeared.

Dinner was a pleasant affair, deliciously cooked and graciously served.

As they left the table, Alex said, "Let's join the kids out back. There's still a couple of hours of daylight left and it's so nice out."

Everyone agreed so the adults were soon ensconced in comfortable lounging chairs while Robbie and Mike decided to play catch.

"Do you miss your trips abroad, Alex?" Greg asked. Alex had not made many trips overseas for the World Relief Organization of which he was a board member since Nathan was a year old. He had decided Nathan needed him at home, at least for these first years of his life.

"Not really," Alex replied. "It was a great help to me when Walter Stuart became a board member, and he and his wife Flora now make most of the trips I was making." Walter Stuart, Janelle Stuart Phillips' father, had been led to the Lord by Alex Harrison's consistent witness by both his transformed lifestyle and his verbal witness. Stuart had recently sold his real estate business in California and moved permanently to Vermont to be near his only child and his three grandchildren.

"Walter Stuart is a living testimony of what the transforming power of God's Holy Spirit can perform in a person's life after one accepts Christ as Saviour," Greg remarked. "He was so against the whole Christian way of life, thinking it was only for people in trouble and those who needed a crutch. The change in him is certainly of the Lord. And, Alex, you didn't give up on him."

"I hardly could," Alex commented dryly. "He was always calling me when he came East. But somehow I always felt that with time and so many praying for him, he would come through sooner or later."

"It's certainly made a difference in Janelle's life," Andrea added.

The conversation turned to generalities and soon Andrea remarked, "We must leave, Greg. It's time Sara and Becky were in bed."

"If Julie can go with you, I believe we'll stay for a bit and chat," Sue said. "Would you like that, John?" she asked her husband.

"Sure thing."

"I'll go along with Robbie, Mom," Mike said.

"Okay. We'll not be too late, Andrea," Sue said.

"Thanks for a lovely evening, Ellyn," Greg smiled as they took their leave.

"You're entirely welcome," Ellyn returned. "See you tomorrow, Andrea."

Sue and John came in around 10:30. Sue remarked smiling, "Plan on fish for dinner tomorrow night, Andrea. John is going fishing with Alex and he also invited Mike, Robbie and Jeffie to go along. It seems Alex has a boat on Lake Champlain. Then we must leave for home early Wednesday morning."

"So soon?" Andrea lamented.

"We want to stop overnight with the folks in White Plains, and Mike has several lawns to mow and care for this summer. Some of them need doing before the weekend."

Soon after the fishermen left the next morning, the phone rang.

"Morning, Andie," Sylvia's voice came over the wire. "How about you and Sue and all the kids coming for lunch? I'll ask Ellyn and Janelle and we can have a gabfest while the kids play."

"Sounds great. Just a minute." Turning to Sue, she said, "Sylvia wants us for lunch, okay?" At Sue's nod, she spoke to Sylvia again. "We'd love to come. What time? Okay, we'll be over."

It was a fun day. An opportunity to enjoy the fellowship for the women, and Anne, Sylvia's twelve-year-old took over the smaller kids while Julie and Janelle's Tricia, who were about the same age, had fun together. That left Jane, Sylvia's youngest, Bede, Janelle's three-year-old, Sara, Becky and Nathan for Anne but she loved it.

"She's a regular little mother, Sylvia," Janelle said.

"Yes, she's a big help to me. She's so serious most of the time, though. It's good for her to loosen up and play with the kids."

Jeffie came rushing in around 3:30 all excited, shouting breathlessly, "We caught our limit and we're all invited to the Harrison's for a fish fry tonight.

Oh boy, was that ever fun!"

"In that case, I guess I'd better get home," Ellyn remarked. "My housekeeper doesn't always accept last-minute plans like this graciously."

"I baked a cake this morning," Sylvia said. "Would you like me to bring that if the invitation is what Jeffie has taken it to be?"

"Mom—!" Jeffie exclaimed, "Grampa Alex said so." He had adopted Robbie's name for Alex Harrison to which Alex always said, "The more the merrier. A big family is what I've always wanted."

"Oh, I expect it's true all right," Ellyn said. "It sounds like Alex and I'd be delighted to have you all." Calling to Nathan to come, she added, "See you all later. Jeffie, did he say what time?"

Jeffie replied, "I think he said around six."

"Okay, see you then."

"Ellyn, I made a macaroni salad this morning. I'll bring that."

"Okay, but it probably won't be necessary."

So the family gathered again that evening at the Harrison estate. It turned out to be baked fish instead of a fish fry. The housekeeper had responded well and made stuffing for the lake trout and salmon. Alex brought home a tub of cole slaw, and with the other contributions it was a smashing success, another good time of family fellowship.

The Thorp family left the following morning soon after Greg did. Robbie ran off to spend the day with his cousin, Jeffie Roberts, and Janelle's son, Ricky Phillips, at Jeffie's house. This left Sara and Becky alone. They fussed a bit so Andrea spent some time letting them help her make cookies. She was making a double batch so that Jason could have some. She did miss having him around the house, although he had kept his promise to drop by every day.

That afternoon, after the girls napped, Andrea decided to go to The Farm to visit her mother and to bring the cookies to Jason.

She found them both at the front desk. Becky immediately jumped up into Jason's lap, giving him a big hug and kiss and demanding, "When you coming home?"

"I'll be by to see you later, Beck, when I'm through here which will be," he said consulting the wall clock, "exactly thirty-six minutes from now."

"I'm through for now, Andrea. Can you stay and talk a few minutes?"

"That's really what I came for, Mom."

Sara took her grandmother's hand and skipped along by her side, chatting away. Andrea had to pry Becky loose from Jason before following.

Once in the family living quarters, the girls were content playing with some toys Nana kept on hand for her grandchildren, while the two women relaxed over a cup of tea.

"When is Cynthia Marsh due to arrive, Mom?" Andrea asked.

"She said she expected to be here on July 8th. She was terminating her present position the 5th. She thought she could make it in two days."

"All set for the Fourth, Mom?"

"Yes, everything seems to be under control, which is a good thing as it's coming up fast now. Jason has been a big help. I do believe he's going to really take to this business."

"I hope so, Mom. I'd like the business to stay in the family and I know Jeff would, too."

"Oh, yes," Lydia replied, "it would really be difficult to let it go after all the hard work we've all put into it."

CHAPTER FOUR

Ken Ross, Jason and Jerry were well settled into the dorm by Monday night. It was a slow week, in some ways, with not more than twenty or so teens, boys and girls, and only nine boys of guest families staying in the dorm. Ken tried to arrange tennis matches for all. There always seemed to be a few couples pairing off, and this week was no exception. At first some newcomers thought croquet a silly game but soon recognized the challenge it provided from skillful players.

Ken was busy arranging his schedule to include an early morning prayer time for any interested guests to attend. He planned an hour of mid-morning Bible study to which everyone was invited. Evenings he organized a variety of programs. Monday was get acquainted night with activities geared to the number of guests. Tuesday night was singalong night, Wednesday was prayer and praise, Thursday was Ken's day off so no meetings were scheduled. Friday night a preaching service and Saturday night a musical by different groups, some local and some from away. Of course, this schedule would have to change during the teen weeks.

Ken was delighted when he learned that Jerry's singing had improved during the year. Jerry admitted he had been in the school choir and had been selected as soloist on many occasions, so Jerry was assigned the task of leading the singalong which pleased him immensely as Gretchen Nelson was the pianist and would be his accompanist.

Ken was amused and Jason was disgusted when Jerry spent every available moment with Gretchen, but undaunted, Jerry agreed to sing often at meetings which frequently threw him into contact with Gretchen. Gretchen also seemed pleased.

The first Friday night Ken looked around the audience and said, "I see some familiar faces from last year, and also some new ones, so I'd like to give my testimony tonight. First of all, I come from a broken home. My dad was an alcoholic and my mother, sickened of the whole deal, left us when I was in my teens. One night in downtown Los Angeles, I was nearly seventeen at the time, I was with a bunch of guys and we were up to no good. We were stealing hubcaps from cars—there was a good market for them. I was just starting to pry one loose on a Cadillac when someone grabbed my arms in a vise-like manner—believe me, I was scared stiff. This was only the second time I'd tried this caper. Then the man asked quietly, 'What are you doing, my boy?'

"I muttered, 'Just lookin'.'

"'Oh? It sure looked like your hands were as busy as your eyes.'

"Just then a cop came close saying, 'Trouble, mister?'"

"'Nothing we can't handle,' the man answered.

"I was stunned and said, 'Why didn't you blow the whistle on me?'

"'It puzzles me why a youngster like you would

be doing something like this. Let's talk, shall we?'

"'You mean . . . you're not gonna turn me in?'

"'Depends. We'll see after we talk.'

"So we talked for nearly four hours. I couldn't believe this man was for real . . . somehow, to my surprise, I opened up to him . . . folks, here was a real man . . . he led me to Christ that night . . . the next day being Sunday we attended church . . . he took me out to eat . . . boy, I'll never forget that meal . . . I hadn't had one like it for sometime . . . next day he took me shopping and bought me some badly needed clothing. In fact, that's what I needed the money for. To make a long story shorter, I promised this man I'd go back to school. When he left he handed me a bill . . . I couldn't believe it! He made me promise to keep in touch with him. I promised, and when I graduated from high school he actually attended my graduation. I had been attending church regularly and felt the Lord leading me into some kind of ministry—to help wayward teens with which our society is teeming. This man offered to pay my way through Bible school, but I wanted to earn at least part of it, so he got me a summer job. I graduated from Bible school, then he asked me if I wanted to attend seminary. I did so we made a deal.

"Then last summer I was asked by the Roberts family to come here. Now I have graduated from seminary and have plans to be ordained this fall. This is all by God's wondrous, marvelous grace, and one of His most loyal servants, folks, was Alex Harrison, the man who has helped me so much. I'll never cease to be grateful to him. He showed me the first love I'd known for years. One more thing, then I promise to close. My father, with whom I kept in touch after I was saved, died last year of cirrhosis of the liver due to alcohol, but I had the privilege of leading him to Christ just before he went into eternity. I don't know where my mother is, but I'm praying that if she is living, she will come to know Him also.

"I'm sorry if I've kept you too long, but one more thing . . . are there any parents here tonight that are not showing their teens and their youngsters a loving attitude by word and deed? Teens and kids, are you being obedient to your parents? Would any of you like to come forward and commit yourselves to a new start? Of course, if you don't know the Saviour, that must be the first step."

Instinctively, Gretchen began playing softly the familiar hymn, 'Just As I Am.'

One couple came forward joined immediately by their teenage son . . . and then others followed.

Jason, who had been sitting with his mother, whispered, "Some guy, eh, and some grandfather I've got! I pray I can be like him someday."

"I pray so, too, son."

Later, Jason remarked to Ken, "I never tire of hearing your testimony. If only more people were like my grandfather, the youth of our generation would have a better chance to make it in this life."

"I agree, Jason. That's one reason I'm in the ministry. I'm looking forward to the teen weeks, especially the inner city work, but I must say I'm relieved that they are bringing their own counselors and leaders. The way I understand it is that nearly all of these kids have attended a mission at least a few times."

"I'm looking forward to that . . . I guess," Jason replied.

Jerry said, "I sure hope we'll be able to cope."

"If we can't, God can, and, of course, that's the only way we have to cope anyway . . . by exercising our faith."

Both boys agreed.

The fourth of July came and went with the usual outdoor barbecue and fireworks. This year a puppet show put on by a young couple was the main attraction and was a great success for both youngsters and adults.

In the afternoon Ken had planned two softball games, one between dads and sons, and the other between moms and daughters. Both proved to be lots of fun. There had been several competitive races planned for the younger children in which Robbie, Jeffie and Anne had been allowed to participate. Cory and Janelle Phillips with their children, Ricky, Tricia and Bede, were there also along with her father Walter Stuart and his wife Flora, who usually joined the Roberts family for the Fourth. All in all, it was a fun day with a patriotic theme worked in, plus the gospel clearly spelled out with the puppet shows.

Jason had been quite disgusted because Jerry hung around with Gretchen all that day, so he allowed himself to be monopolized by one of the guests, Sheila Morrell. Sheila had been coming to The Farm with her family for two years now and she tagged along behind Jason when he had worked outside the past two years until he finally accepted her as a friend. This year she started hanging around the office until Lydia hinted strongly that it was not appropriate, therefore, she was radiant when Jason seemed friendly that day.

The following morning Jerry casually remarked, "I've been invited to the Nelsons' for dinner on Thursday. That's my day off, you know."

Jason stared at him before nonchalantly replying, "One thing I know, you'll have a good meal."

Jerry answered dreamily, "I expect, but that's not the main reason . . . Gretchen is coming in early today so we can practice for Saturday night. We're having the young people's quartet from your church and Ken asked me to sing a couple of solos."

Jason said, "Hey, that's good, Jere. You planning a musical career?"

"I just might. Gretchen is, you know. She plans

to be a music teacher," he answered, trying to remain casual.

"I can see this summer is going to be different than last year, all right," Jason remarked dryly.

"What was that? What did you say?"

"Nothing, pal, nothing important anyway. Well, I have to be off to work. See ya."

So it came about that Jason promised Sheila that he would play tennis with her after work that afternoon, and discovered that it wasn't half that bad having a girl hang on your every word.

Jerry waxed eloquent about his trip to the Nelson home. They stopped by Kurt's farm market so Jerry could meet Gretchen's older brother and his family.

"They really have something going there, Jase. Hard work, as Kurt says, but you can tell that both he and his wife, Lisa, love it. They sure have two cute kids, Eddie and Robin, I believe she said. The younger brother helps out occasionally when his father can spare him. All of them appear to be a super family. I can see why Gretchen is such a lovely girl . . . besides her graceful appearance and beautiful hair."

Jason only said, "I agree about the Nelsons. Kurt and Lisa are special friends of mine. I worked with them one summer at The Farm here when we had our own garden. In fact, the garden was on this exact spot where the dorm is now. Hey, did you know we are contemplating putting up another dorm for girls for next year?"

"Where do you get the 'we' stuff?" Jerry teased.

With a slight shrug, Jason replied, "I hope to become actively involved in our family business when I get older. This year is my actual initiation into everything it includes."

Placing a hand on his friend's shoulder, Jerry said, "I was only teasing, Jase, I know how serious you are about this business, and I don't blame you. It's turned out to be quite a ministry, hasn't it?

By the way, where do you plan to attend college?"

"I'm not sure yet. Someplace where I can get both business administration and Bible."

"Lots of decisions at our age, eh, friend?"

"At any age it seems," was Jason's reply. "Look at Ken. The decisions he made at our age made all the difference in his life."

"Right you are," Jerry agreed.

"See you later," Jason said, hurrying off to work. That afternoon Jason stopped by his home to see Becky and the family. As usual, Andrea had prepared some food for him to take back with him. This time it was cupcakes.

As he was leaving, he said, "Well, I suppose the Marsh girl is due to arrive Saturday. All I remember about her was her gorgeous red hair."

"That is something to remember, but I'm sure she has other qualities."

"But she's not saved, Mom."

"No, but we're all praying for her. I hope you guys are, too."

"I'll remind 'em tonight. See you all later." Giving Becky and Sara a kiss, he left. As he went out the door he met Robbie coming in. "How goes it, Rob?"

"Okay, Jeff and I am having fun down by the brook building a dam."

"Playing beaver, eh? Well, have fun. See ya," he called over his shoulder. "Thanks for the cupcakes, Mom."

"You're entirely welcome, son."

"Cupcakes!" Robbie exclaimed. "Can I have one, Mom?"

"Just one for now. They are for dessert tonight."

"Okay," he said, grabbing one. With his mouth full, he exclaimed, "Yummy, Mom, yummy. Call me when dinner is ready."

This family of mine is sure growing and changing she thought as Greg's car drove in and the girls flew out the door calling, "Daddy's home."

The thought flowed through her mind ... I wonder if having Cynthia Marsh around will bring any changes into our lives, but the thought vanished as quickly as it came when she happily welcomed her husband home from work.

CHAPTER FIVE

Early the morning of July 7th in a small city in the southwestern section of Pennsylvania, Cynthia Marsh was just putting the last of her night things in a tote bag. She hoped she would only have to stay over one night on her way to Vermont.

Her mother appeared in the doorway of her bedroom just as she was closing the zipper.

"All packed?" her mother asked.

"Guess so. I hope I haven't forgotten anything."

"You're sure you are doing the right thing, running off to Vermont?"

Cynthia stared at her, then shrugged her shoulders. "No, I'm not sure but it's something to do. And I have to get away."

"Well, I hope you won't get involved in Matt's religion. You could turn out as deluded as you have with Ted Blacks."

"I'd rather not discuss it," was Cynthia's blunt answer.

"You know what my philosophy of life is . . ."

"Very well, Mother," she interrupted. "You believe that one has to accept what comes along in life and adjust to it the best you can."

Cynthia and her mother had never had the best of a relationship. Her mother was the domineering type who ruled her husband with an iron thumb and thought she ruled her son, Oliver, as well.

"I don't know why you won't be like Oliver, he's never given me any trouble."

"Now, Mother, what real trouble have I ever given you?" Cynthia demanded.

"None, I guess, except your stubbornness in listening to my guidance."

"Let's face it, you've always been more interested in Oliver and your bridge parties. I've always felt everything in your life came before me . . . or even before Dad."

"You've no cause to be impudent, my girl, and have you ever heard your father complain?"

"He wouldn't dare," Cynthia muttered.

"Well, I certainly hope you fit into this wonderful family Matt brags so much about."

"At least one thing I know from the one week I spent there five years ago, they are all loving, caring people and right now that's what I need. I'd better get going. I want to get there by tomorrow night."

"All right, but I've made some blueberry muffins and I hope you'll have the decency to take time to eat some."

Cynthia was momentarily touched. Her mother seldom catered to her but why did she have to spoil it by speaking as she had? Oliver always came first. Blueberry muffins were one of her favorites and Oliver disliked them, so it was a surprise to learn her mother had made them just for her. "Ummm, sounds good. Dad gone?"

"No, he's waiting to say good-bye to you. Oliver has gone but he said to say so long."

Cynthia followed her mother to the kitchen

where her dad was just finishing his breakfast. Blueberry muffins were one of his favorites, too, so he was silently enjoying them.

"Morning, Dad."

"Good morning, Cindy. You all packed?"

"Yup, all ready to start as soon as I have one of these delicious-looking muffins and a cup of coffee."

She finished eating just as her father pushed his chair away from the table. Rising she said, "Guess I'd better be on my way. Thanks for the muffins, Mother."

"You're welcome, I'm sure," was her mother's stiff reply.

"Well, I guess it's good-bye then," Cynthia said.

"Here, let me take your bag," her dad said as he reached for it.

Relinquishing it, Cynthia gave her mother a quick glance.

"Good-bye, Cynthia. Now don't pick up any hitchhikers."

Cynthia laughed, "Don't worry, Mother, I won't," then followed her father out to the car.

Cynthia's car was in the driveway. Her dad opened the door of the two-door Festiva and placed her bag on the rear seat. Then he followed her around to the driver's side. As she opened the car door, she was surprised when he put his arm around her shoulder and bent to kiss her on the cheek. A display of any affection was rarely seen in the Marsh household.

"Remember, Cindy, I love you. I've always been proud of you, and I'm sorry you've had an unhappy life thus far."

She stared at him. She had never realized that he really cared for her except he had taken her side a time or two when she and Oliver had been fighting, and when they were little he had taken them both, on scant occasion, to a circus or to the zoo.

41

"Thanks, Dad," she whispered. Then abruptly she asked, "Why do you let Mother boss you around so much, Dad? Do you really love her?"

"Of course I do, child. She's basically a good wife and mother."

"How can you say that when she never—but never seems to care what pleases **you**?"

"That's not entirely true, Cindy. I've always had my comfortable chair, my slippers and good meals."

"But she caters to Oliver first," Cynthia persisted.

"Well," he shrugged, "I'm not fussy."

"She leaves you alone so much at night for her bridge parties. Doesn't that bother you?"

Surprising her with a slight twinkle in his eyes, he replied in a mild tone, "I have my T.V. and my newspapers, and peacefulness, those times. But, seriously, Cindy, take care now, and you will write, won't you?"

"Of course I will, Dad, if you really want me to."

"I do. I'm glad you're going to your Uncle Matt. I've liked what little I've seen of him. And Kate, too. If you don't like it there, remember you're always welcome here."

"You think Mother would welcome me back?"

"Now, child, don't go away bearing a grudge against her, or any of us. We're all the family you have, you know, and I'm sure your mother is fond of you."

"You could have fooled me . . ."

"Well, I must go now or I'll be late for work."

As Cynthia backed her car out of the driveway, she waved to her father and thought she caught a glimpse of her mother in the kitchen window.

Cynthia thought about her father as she weaved her way through the traffic of the morning rush hour. She knew her father brought home a good paycheck as foreman in the machine shop where he worked. She wondered briefly how he could have risen to the position of foreman with his retiring nature. All at once she thought it might have been interesting to have visited him there. No doubt he wasn't the same person on the job as at home or he couldn't be in charge of other men. Then her thoughts were drawn away from her family as she concentrated on catching the right ramp to the thruway.

Her mind was occupied all day, keeping her Festiva in the right lane and trying to keep within the speed limit. She drove off around noon to grab a bite to eat and buy gas. At seven o'clock she drove into Binghamton, New York. Catching sight of an attractive motel sign, she followed directions the short distance to the motel, becoming dismayed when she observed so many cars. Inquiring at the reservation desk, she found a friendly clerk who said, "You're a lucky lady, we have one room left."

"I'll take it," she said with relief.

Her attention was drawn to the dining room as she made a quick decision to eat something before she went to her room. She didn't linger over her meal and on her way out she bought a magazine to help pass away the evening hours.

Locating her parking space, she grabbed her tote bag, locked her car and climbed the iron steps to her third-floor room. She unlocked the door, tossed her bag onto a nearby chair, and locked and bolted her door again.

Next she drew the drapes across the window and decided to take a shower and get into her nightclothes. She wanted to be as fresh as possible when she arrived at The Farm.

As the full force of water hit her she realized all at once how tense she was. Turning, she let the spray hit the nape of her neck to relax her. Finally toweled and robed, she stepped back into the room. All of a sudden she slumped forward as wave after wave of despair enveloped her body, soul and spirit.

Rushing to the bed she flung herself face downward as she burst into a torrent of tears. She hadn't shed a tear up until now.

She wailed aloud, "Teddy—oh, Teddy, why did you leave me? I loved you so much. How could you do this to me!" Her mind was being buffeted about like a tumbleweed on a windswept desert. She recalled his good-bye note vividly as though every word were etched on her memory forever. "It would never work, Cynthia, I have been fearful for some weeks now that you are too weak for me, that you consider me your god instead of realizing that you are a god yourself; therefore, we could not work together to change the world. Ethel is as strong as I am. We'll make a great team. I sincerely hope you have grasped enough of my teaching so that you will find enough strength within yourself to go on with your life. All the best, Ted."

She recalled more vividly the day she had met Ted Black. He was holding a meeting in one of the hotel's meeting rooms where she was employed. She had been so attracted by his dark good looks, his wavy black hair, sharp black eyes, his magnetic personality, that she had slipped into a back seat as he was speaking. She was mesmerized by his appearance and fell madly, blindly in love with him. She recalled faintly what he was saying, he had been so sure of himself.

"I was made in the image of God, therefore, I am like God, therefore, I am a god." He had been so arrogant as he used phrases such as: each person individually needed to find their own highest potential . . . they needed to get in touch with the god within themselves . . . she faintly recalled him saying self-awareness, and other words. She believed every word he had spoken. After the meeting people lingered to talk with each other and Ted approached Cynthia with his captivating smile asking, "How did you like what you heard? I've never seen you at a meeting before, have I?"

She stammered, "No, you haven't, and I think you are absolutely marvelous."

"But how about my concepts?" he prodded.

"Oh, they sound wonderful."

"Would you like to join our group?" he invited.

"Oh, yes," she gushed.

"How about having dinner with me and I'll fill you in on our meeting plans, our goals, life, and so forth."

"I'd love that," she answered breathlessly, gazing adoringly at him.

From that moment on he had taken all her free time and she had fallen into his trap, so now she wailed again, "Oh, Teddy, my only weakness was in loving you so much."

Suddenly it dawned upon her as she lay feeling debilitated and spent after weeping so violently. "He was my god. I never did discover one within myself. But he was all I needed . . . I thought . . ." But once again the familiar feeling of bitterness engulfed her . . . the feeling she had been living with for these past weeks . . . the bitterness she felt as she canceled all her wedding arrangements and discovered that there would be no refunds on deposits she had made.

"Oh, what's the use of anything . . . of even living . . . I wonder if I'll always be rejected by people . . . even my family . . . except for this morning when my father told me he loved me. Bitterness once again crept over her as she cried out, "Why didn't he ever tell me that before! It could have made such a difference in my life . . . Teddy was the only one to show me love and now he's gone . . . what's the use of living . . . that's it . . . I won't . . . jumping from the bed she grabbed her tote bag and groped for the over-the-counter sleeping pills she had bought to help her sleep the past few nights.

Rushing to the bathroom she filled a paper cup with water . . . emptying the contents of the bottle into the palm of her hand she raised it to her mouth, and as she did so she caught a glimpse of herself in the mirror. Horrified, she thought—I look like a wild person. Looking at the pills she shuddered as long forgotten words gripped her thoughts. Words she had heard five years ago when she had visited Uncle Matt and Aunt Kate in Vermont. She had attended a church service with them . . . the speaker had talked about heaven and hell as being real places and one had to choose which one they would spend eternity in . . . trembling, she dropped the pills and water and stumbled back to her bed. Dare she take that chance . . . what if that preacher were right . . . Uncle Matt seemed to think so. Trembling more violently at the terrible tragedy she had almost committed, she thought despairingly . . . one thing Ted was right about, I am weak . . . there is no inner strength or resource within me to fall back on. Suddenly she felt empty . . . void . . . as if some vital part of her were missing. Shaking herself she muttered, "But I must go on . . . somehow, I must make a new life for myself." Resting her head on the pillow she felt an utter sense of weariness deaden her being . . . lying inert, she finally drifted off to sleep.

There was no way for her to know that a few minutes ago her Uncle Matt had wakened his wife and said, "Kate, I can't sleep. I feel a heavy sense of burden that Cynthia is in deep trouble right now. Will you pray with me?"

Sliding to their knees beside the bed they poured out their heart to their burden-bearer. "Oh, Heavenly Father," Matt prayed, "I feel Cynthia needs protection from some awful calamity right now. Will You please intervene and protect her from any harm. I do want so much for her to know You."

Kate prayed also and finally they went back into bed with a feeling of relief that all was in the Father's hands . . . Matt felt the relief that came to a burdened soul after leaving his problems in

His control.

In Binghamton, New York, Cynthia slept, not even realizing she had been committed into God's keeping by a loving uncle and aunt.

CHAPTER SIX

Cynthia slept later than she intended to so when she woke she had to rush around, which didn't leave her time to dwell on the events of the night before. When she stepped outside the door though, she breathed deeply of the fresh air, really grateful to be alive. She shuddered when she thought of what she had nearly done. Maybe, after all, her mother's philosophy was right, to make the best of life as it came your way, but somehow that idea brought scant comfort.

After a hasty breakfast she headed north. It was a lovely July day, a perfect day for traveling. Except for a brief time getting the right route at the Albany exit, things went well with the trip. As she neared Burlington she stopped at a wayside parking place to scan Uncle Matt's directions carefully. They didn't seem difficult and she was accustomed to city driving.

She pulled into the parking lot at The Farm at exactly 4:45 p.m. Climbing out of her car she stretched and looked around. It all seemed vaguely familiar. Just then a young man appeared from the front entrance and called, "Miss Marsh?"

"Yes, it's me," she answered cautiously.

Taking long strides, he advanced to her side in no time. Holding out his hand he said, "Hi. Welcome to The Farm. I'm Jason Holloway."

She stared at him. "But . . ." she stammered, "you were only about so tall . . . but, of course, that was five years ago. How do I find Uncle Matt, Jason?"

Uncle Matt answered that question himself, as he appeared around the corner of the motel. "Well, I see you made it okay, Cindy. I'm so glad to see you." Bending, he kissed her lightly on the cheek. "Still got that gorgeous red hair, I see." All the time he was observing her face which showed traces of pinched lines, evidence of her hurting. "Come now, let's unload your luggage. Kate is anxiously waiting to see you."

"Let me help," Jason offered. "If you'll give me the keys to your trunk, Miss Marsh, I'll take some of your luggage."

"I only have to press a button in here," she replied, leaning into the car and pressing the button which released the lock on the trunk door.

"Neat," Jason said, lifting stuff out. "Now then, Mr. A., I'll carry it in. Second floor by your room, right?"

"Right," replied Matt. "I'll bring the rest of it." Turning to his niece he said, "Better lock your car."

"Here?" she asked astonished.

"Yes, here. Not that we think our guests are unreliable, but one never knows. Even though we are off the main highway, many cars get lost and turn in here."

"Okay, if you say so."

"You can leave the car here for now, but you'll be keeping it over at the garage with the other vehicles of live-in help. Come now, let's go inside. Bet you're tired."

"Yes, I'm tired. It's a long trip. But I'm okay. It seems good to be here. So nice and peaceful."

Matt grinned. "Not always as quiet as right now."

They met Jason coming down the stairs as they went up and Kate was waiting in the hallway door. "Welcome, Cynthia. My, it's good to see you again." Her aunt held both hands out to grasp hers. Her gentle touch lightened Cynthia's heart.

"Here," Kate said, leading the way into the first room at the right. "This is where Mrs. Roberts has put you for now. We are just across the hall. When you are ready, come to our apartment for supper. We often eat here. We thought you might like it better tonight with just us rather than a lot of strangers."

"That's thoughtful of you, Aunt Kate. I appreciate it. I'll be over soon."

"I'll go down to the kitchen and get the food. It will be ready in half an hour. Okay?"

"Sounds fine to me," Cynthia smiled wanly. As the door closed behind Kate, she looked around her room. Lovely, she thought. Exploring further, she discovered a roomy closet and her own bathroom. Opening her largest bag, she shook out garments and put them away. She then unpacked her cosmetic bag and arranged these articles in the bathroom and on her dresser.

After washing her face and hands and running a comb through her hair, she went across the hallway. At her tap, Kate called, "Come in."

As Cynthia entered the room, Kate was putting the meal on the table. "It's just hot roast beef sandwiches tonight, but we have some of our delicious cole slaw to go with it, and I have fresh strawberry shortcake for dessert."

"Sounds good," Cynthia answered, then added, "you have every convenience here, don't you?" as she observed the area that could be closed off with sliding doors and took in the sink, counter space, microwave oven and small appliances with a miniature refrigerator under the counter top.

"Yes, we have all we need when we want to be by ourselves for meals, which is most of the time. We do, however, nearly always get the food from the kitchen, which is all prepared. The Roberts family is very considerate of us."

"Well, you have given them loyal service for years," Cynthia commented.

"True, but they still wouldn't have to do this for us," Kate answered. "Come on, let's eat before the gravy gets cold."

After they were seated, Cynthia started to pick up her fork before she remembered that Uncle Matt prayed before they ate. She bowed her head with them as he prayed: "Heavenly Father, we thank You for bringing our niece safely here. We pray that during her time of hurting, she may come to know You who has bid those who have need to 'come unto me, all ye that labor and are heavy-laden, and I will give you rest. Take my yoke upon you, and learn of me; for I am meek and lowly in heart: and ye shall find rest for your souls. For my yoke is easy and my burden is light.'

"We thank You for this food and for every provision of comfort You have given us. I pray that Cynthia might enjoy her work and her time here with us. In Jesus name, Amen."

The air was slightly tense for a few seconds until Matt asked, "Did you have a nice trip?"

"So-so," she answered succinctly.

"How are all of your family?" was his next question.

"About the same," then, feeling she wasn't being exactly friendly to these kind relatives, she added, "Mother keeps busy with her bridge parties and catering to Oliver."

"And your dad?"

"The same, but you know, I used to think Dad was as unhappy as I was at home but something he said the day I left led me to believe he is at least content."

"And Oliver?"

"He's doing okay. He is a car salesman. In fact, he helped me get a good deal on my Festiva."

"I noticed you had a neat little car," her uncle added.

Cynthia shrugged. "It gets me where I want to go."

They had finished the meal by then and she asked, "Do we wash the dishes here, Aunt Kate?"

"Yes, but it will only take a minute."

"Would you like to go to the service in the chapel with us tonight?" Matt asked.

With a startled look, Cynthia answered quickly, "Oh, no, not tonight. I'm beat. When do I meet with Mrs. Roberts?"

Kate answered, "She said Monday morning is fine."

"I believe I'll go to my room now and finish unpacking. See you both in the morning."

"We usually eat breakfast here in our apartment. Why don't you eat with us tomorrow, Cindy?"

"Thanks, I will. What time?"

"We usually eat around eight on Sundays. Matt likes to take a look around to see that everything is okay and to check at the front desk for any problems. Church here at the chapel is at 11:00 o'clock. Sunday school is at 9:45. We attend both services."

"Will I be expected to attend all services in the chapel while I'm here?"

"None of it is compulsory, but we hope you will want to go," her uncle replied.

As Cynthia started to open the door to the hallway, Matt said, "Cindy, we are delighted to have you with us. I want you to know that we care deeply for you. I've mentioned to Kate several times that if we had had a daughter, I'd have liked her to be just like you."

"That goes for me, too," Kate added gently.

Matt cleared his throat. With his taciturn nature, she could tell it was difficult for him to express himself. "I know you haven't had the best of a home life. Kate and I would like to make it as pleasant as possible here for you. How would it be if you considered us as . . . parents for now . . . we are here for you when you need us . . . ready to listen . . . and help . . ."

Cynthia, near tears, turned and said huskily, "I really appreciate your caring, Uncle Matt . . . Aunt Kate. I can't talk about it now . . . maybe I can later. It's all just too close to me yet . . ." She stumbled on haltingly, "I'm trying to sort it all out in my mind . . . okay?"

"Cynthia, did you have any trouble . . . problems last night?"

Startled, she said, "Not really . . . or at least I can't talk about it now . . . I'm trying to leave it in the past. But why do you ask?"

With a quick look at his wife and her slight shake of the head, he answered with his shy smile, "Maybe we can talk about that sometime, also."

"I really do appreciate all you are offering me. I just need a little time right now."

"All the time you need, Cindy," Kate responded. "For now, if you need anything in your room just let me know. Have a good night, dear."

Almost overwhelmed by so much kindness, Cynthia opened the door, saying softly, "Good night."

Once in her room she busied herself unpacking and stowing her things away in the closet and bureau. After her luggage was emptied, she pushed it into the closet and closed the door. Turning back to the room, the same feeling of despair flooded her soul. Frantically she thought, what am I doing in this out of the way place, anyway! . . . why didn't I have the courage to stay home . . . then she remembered her relatives' kind greeting which lifted her spirits a bit. Resolutely she undressed, showered and got ready for bed. She felt totally exhausted. Once in bed, she remembered she hadn't brushed her hair ... but what does it matter ... but it had been a habit of hers for so long, she couldn't settle down.

Climbing wearily out of bed she reached for her brush and methodically counted, one, two, three ... keeping strictly at it until the exact count of one hundred. It had relaxed her so that she drifted instantly into sleep when she went back to bed.

When she awoke the next morning, the sun was streaming brightly into her face. A faint breeze was moving the drapes at the windows she had left open to the night air. Feeling still tired, she moved languidly, then suddenly sat upright thinking, what time is it? Snatching her watch from the bedside table, she felt horrified. Eleven o'clock! Oh, dear, what will they think of me?

Jumping out of bed, she splashed water over her sleep-swollen eyelids and quickly dressed. As she was about to leave her room she stopped short. Of course, Uncle Matt and his wife would be in church. She decided to go to their room and see, anyway. Sure enough, the door was locked but there was a note attached telling her they would be back soon after twelve and would like to take her out for Sunday dinner and a drive if she felt up to it.

She returned slowly to her room. How nice of them to make plans to entertain her today ... her heart which seemed forever to be yearning for someone to care was deeply touched.

She took special pains to look her best, thinking this would please her relatives. She chose a white pique sleeveless dress and a short light blue bolero jacket with matching shoes. She was just putting on her white earrings when a knock sounded on her door. Moving quickly, she opened it. Uncle Matt stood there in his Sunday suit with a broad smile.

"All set, Cindy? Kate is waiting in the car.

Did you have a nice sleep?"

"Just great, Uncle Matt. I'm sorry I overslept. You mustn't think I do that often, because I don't."

"That's okay. We thought perhaps you would. Kate felt badly because she hadn't given you a key to our apartment. I'll bet you're starved."

She smiled at him. "I am a bit hungry."

"You like seafood?"

"Love it," she replied.

As they reached the car, Kate called a greeting, "My you look lovely, Cindy. Did you sleep well?"

"Yes, Aunt Kate. I love my room and I do appreciate the warm welcome you two have given me. I only hope I can do the tasks that will be assigned to me."

"Don't worry about that, my dear. The Roberts family is easy to work for."

It was an enjoyable afternoon. After a delectable dinner, they traveled over several highways, the Andersons pointing out places of interest.

Once back at The Farm, Matt asked Cynthia if she would like to attend the evening chapel service with them. She was about to say no when she detected a wistful look in her uncle's eyes, so reluctantly she agreed to go with them.

She was surprised to find the building nearly full of people of all ages. A young man whom Aunt Kate whispered was Jason's cousin sang beautifully, accompanied by a young lady with silvery blonde hair. They both seemed so sincere in their efforts.

When the speaker arose from his chair behind the podium, she stared . . . the blonde young man looked more like an athlete than a preacher. She wondered if he would talk about heaven and hell as the minister had five years ago when she was visiting her relatives. Somehow she hoped he would, in her innermost being she felt an urgency to know more about that subject. She had so recently had such a narrow escape.

He opened his Bible and announced that his

text was from Ephesians, chapter two. He then said, "I'd like to speak on what I'm sure are familiar verses to some of you, but it never hurts to remind ourselves that we are saved by grace alone," quoting, "For by grace are ye saved through faith, it is the gift of God, not of works lest any man should boast."

At the word boast, Cynthia's thoughts flashed instantly to Ted. All he had ever done was boast. He never drank intoxicating beverages because, as he had said, he needed always to be in command of his thoughts and actions to reach his highest potential; the same with smoking, it could injure his body. He scorned drugs as the quickest way to destroy oneself. As for immoral acts, he wanted to protect his body from all diseases, all to reach his highest potential as a god. He was so arrogant in his ways, and only tolerated those around him who were weaker because it made him feel stronger. She thought bitterly . . . I followed his ideals, and where did it get me! Rejected—abandoned—but then, I'm glad now that I didn't succumb to some of the practices of the group. Ted had lectured them severely, and some of them really tried, but for some reason just couldn't be consistent.

Her thoughts were jerked abruptly to the present as the young preacher said, "Amen," evidently the end of the sermon. He announced a hymn, and as the congregation sang, "My hope is built on nothing less than Jesus' blood and righteousness," she glanced at those nearest her and observed their apparent sincerity, and the vigor with which they sang, as though it were straight from the heart. Even Uncle Matt was following along in a slightly off-key tone. What would it be like to have inner peace like these people seemed to have . . . her heart felt heavy with a deep longing for something . . . she hoped that here she would not be rejected . . . she knew her relatives accepted and appeared fond of her . . . but would the Roberts family accept her for what she was, and be as kind as she remembered them?

As they left the chapel, they met Lydia Roberts. Matt introduced them and Cynthia's spirits lifted a bit more at Lydia's warm welcome as she clasped both hands and said with a smile, "Welcome, Cynthia. I'm so glad to meet you again and am looking forward to working with you. How about meeting me at the front desk at eight tomorrow morning and we'll discuss your duties."

"I'll be there," Cynthia said, thinking, she seems so very kind.

As she parted from her uncle and aunt in the hallway, Kate handed her a key. Here's a key for you to our apartment. We usually eat breakfast early as we both try to be on the job early, Matt at 7:00 and me at 7:30. You can either eat here or in the dining room. In any event, we'd like you to have a key so that if you want a cup of tea or coffee by yourself, or whatever, when we're not here . . ."

Cynthia surprised herself and them by flinging her arms around their necks and giving them both a kiss on the cheek. "You two are so good to me . . . you'll never know how much it means to me . . . especially right now in my life."

As she turned to her own door, she felt again the deep yearning of her heart to be loved and accepted for what she was, not for what others wanted her to be . . . and at least Uncle Matt and Aunt Kate were doing just that. As she inserted the key into the lock, her heart felt lighter than it had in weeks. Maybe . . . just maybe . . . she would find happiness here at The Farm.

CHAPTER SEVEN

Cynthia was up early the next morning. She wanted to look her best this first day on the job. Choosing a belted skirt of jade green with a matching blouse which accentuated her slim waist, she added matching earrings and slipped a jade ring on her finger. Meticulously brushing her heavy head of hair, she felt grateful that it had a natural wave and was of such a good texture—she could style it almost any way she chose. Brushing it away from her face, she decided to let it fall into its natural waves today which usually ended in wispy curls forming around her hairline.

Leaning closer to the mirror she noticed her face was less drawn and her soft brown eyes were not as distressed, thinking, I already feel less tense here. Satisfied that she had done her best as far as her appearance was concerned, she locked her door and joined her uncle and aunt for a light breakfast, after which Kate showed her the way to the front office.

Cynthia arrived promptly almost to the minute. Lydia Roberts was already there, busy looking over some papers.

At Cynthia's rather shy, "Good morning, Mrs. Roberts," she looked up smiling.

"Good morning, Cynthia, you're right on time. I like that. It's a good beginning."

"I always make it a point to be on time," Cynthia replied a bit uneasily.

Lydia pulled a chair up beside her and said, "Here, sit by me and we'll talk. I'm just about finished with my work for today." Looking at the clock, she said, "Jason's late . . . again. He knows I don't like that. When he does get here, we'll go to my living quarters. In the meantime, would you tell me exactly what your duties were in your last position and . . ."

"Mornin', Nan," Jason appeared almost on the run. "Mornin', Miss Marsh."

Glancing significantly at the wall clock, his grandmother said, "Late again, Jason. You know I don't like that. If it happens once more we'll talk with your parents and then if it continues, well, we'll see . . ."

"Aw, Nan, I intended to be here earlier but . . ."

"Jason, I don't like excuses. Unless you are ill, I expect you to be on time . . . is that understood?"

Jason blushed in obvious embarrassment and meekly replied, "Yes, ma'am, but . . ."

"Just be here on time from now on, okay?"

"Okay, but Nan, don't be so hard on a guy," he said, wrapping his arm around her shoulders. "Forgive me?"

"Jason, you'll get nowhere with all that charm," she replied, melting somewhat.

"Okay, okay, I get the message. See ya later, Miss Marsh."

Cynthia glanced back at him as she followed Lydia down the hallway. He winked and brought his hand up in a quick salute. She grinned back.

As they made their way to the family living quarters, Lydia pointed out the main lounge and passing through the dining room she greeted several guests and the hostess, introducing Cynthia as the new assistant manager.

Entering the kitchen she also met the cooks and received a cordial welcome. It did seem as though this was going to be a pleasant place to work after all . . .

"Would you like some coffee, Cynthia? I'm having some."

"Yes, that sounds good."

Taking their cups to the living room, Lydia seated herself at the gate-legged table and motioned for Cynthia to join her. "Now then, you were about to tell me what your duties consisted of in your last position."

"In name, I was assistant manager. In actuality, I was more like a social director. I had charge of all the meeting rooms. We had several clubs that met at the hotel. I had to meet with the one in charge and take care of 'details'."

"Such as?" Lydia inquired.

"If food was required, a luncheon, full meal or just a snack, I was responsible for that, plus seating arrangements and things of that nature. Occasionally I filled in at the reservation desk."

"You liked your work?"

"Very much."

"I've been thinking of how you could help me to the best advantage. My family has been after me for some time now to take it easier. We need someone in the office nearly all the time, mostly for emergencies. Jason is on days from 8:00 to 4:00. We have a young man from church, Don Noble, who comes in at night, but he doesn't come in until 6:00 and he leaves at 6:00 in the morning. He's working his way through college and has a daytime job as well. My father-in-law and I have been taking turns filling in the odd hours. Would you mind taking those shifts every other day, for now anyway?"

"I think I'd like that."

"Then, I'd like you to sort of get acquainted in every area. One day a week I need someone to take the dining room hostess's place . . . her day off . . . ever done that?"

"Yes . . . not many times, but I'm willing to learn."

"Good girl," Lydia smiled. "Now then, we have a new venture this year. We have five weeks of teen boys coming into the dorm. The week after next is the first week. I'd like you to go over there and talk with Ken Ross, the chaplain, who is in charge, and find out about food and so forth. He'll show you around. It would relieve me immensely to have someone to share these responsibilities. Now . . . how about your taking the desk shifts Monday, Wednesday and Friday, starting tonight?"

"What do I have to do?"

"If you go out now, Jason will show you the reservation listing. It might be a good idea if you browse around this week and get acquainted with the buildings. Kate will show you around this building. Then Gramps, that's my father-in-law but everyone calls him Gramps, will show you the efficiencies in the other building. Also, we have a snack bar open 10:00 till 10:00. It would help if you could keep track of the needs there, also. I do all of the food ordering, perhaps you can help me with that later. Sound like too much?"

"Oh, no. I think I'll like the varied routine."

"Okay then, I need to get busy. I haven't seen you in the dining room yet. Your meals go with your job. You'll have one day off a week. Oh, yes, we need to talk wages."

They reached an amiable agreement before Lydia rose and said, "I'll see you later. Just look around and be sure to relieve Jason at 4:00. About dinner, you can eat either before or after. I'm so pleased to have you here, Cynthia. I do hope you'll like it. Matt and Kate seem overjoyed to have you. They are really great people."

"I'm finding that out," Cynthia agreed as they parted.

Arriving back at the office, she found Jason busy admitting a family. She stepped to the side and watched him as he dealt with the arrangements. Evidently these people had been here before as Jason seemed to know them.

"We have a few changes this year. Ken Ross is back and has set up a new routine of meetings. The schedule is listed on the bulletin board and also on the insert in your brochure." Handing them the room key, he added, "Guess you know the way. Have a nice week, now. And remember, we're here to help you do just that." As the guests departed, Jason turned to Cynthia.

"You did that very nicely, Jason," she remarked.

"Oh, well, I was brought up here, you know. This is my first year of being on my own." His face flushed slightly as he said, "About this morning . . ."

"Never mind," she replied, "I do not want to get involved in any family business but, young man," she cautioned with a smile, "you'd better be on time the days I'm on early shift . . . or else!"

"Or else what?" Jason said a trifle impudently. "Seriously, Miss Marsh . . ."

"Please call me Cynthia . . . if it's permitted."

He replied doubtfully, "I'm not sure that my grandmother will approve."

"Okay. Now show me . . ." and they talked business routines for half an hour or so.

"Thanks, Jason, I'll see you at four . . . sharp!" she grinned.

Locating Kate in the second floor linen closet, together they made a survey of the linens which were neatly labeled and arrayed. "You probably will be called on to supply clean linen sometime or other . . . like extra towels . . . crib sheets, etc. . . .

although the guests usually want those things later in the evening or at night. Anyway, it keeps Don busy."

At noontime Cynthia decided to eat in the dining room to get acquainted with the hostess and observe the routine there. Helping herself from the salad bar, she found a table alone and quietly observed as she ate. Ummm, the food is delicious . . . I'll have to watch my weight, she thought.

Just as she was finishing, the hostess slid onto a chair across from her. "Lydia tells me you'll be taking my place on my day off . . . which is Friday this week . . . Lydia is kind enough to let me have whatever day I want . . . in fact, some weeks I take two days." Indicating the waitresses she said, "Some of these girls are new, but I guess I have managed to train them . . . the older girls are extremely efficient." Arising abruptly, she added, "Gotta go . . . see you later. Glad you're with us. Hope you like it here."

"Thanks. I'm sure I will," Cynthia replied.

After lunch, she went to find Mrs. Roberts' father-in-law. Going through the kitchen, she asked one of the cooks where he might be located.

"He's probably in their apartment at this time of day."

Going through the hallway, she tapped on the door. A pleasant voice called, "Come in." As she entered, a silver-haired man with a slight build rose from his chair and extended his hand to her. "Cynthia Marsh?" he inquired, smiling.

"Yes . . . but how did you guess?"

"By your red hair," he answered. "I'm Gramps. Lydia asked me if I'd show you around the efficiency apartments."

"That's next on my list," she told him.

"Okay, let's go out this way," he replied. Leading the way, he explained, "This used to be the barn but we remodeled it a few years ago. Let me introduce you to the snack bar attendant," he said as they arrived at the building. Sliding glass windows stretched across the front for service. There were a couple of giggling teenage girls waiting for an order. "It should be only a few minutes, Miss Marsh."

"Please call me Cynthia," she said as the girls departed with huge ice cream sundaes.

Stepping forward, Gramps said, "Donna, I'd like you to meet Cynthia Marsh. She's Mrs. Roberts' new assistant. Cynthia, Donna Fisher."

"Hi, Donna. I noticed the hours you're open are from 10:00 to 10:00. Do you work all that time?"

"No," Donna replied in a friendly manner, "my older sister Joan comes in at five. Mrs. Roberts told me I would contact you for the food needs. I have a list here I need for tomorrow. Would you like it now?"

"Yes, please. I'll be in touch later, Donna."

"Nice to meet you, Miss Marsh," Donna replied with a friendly smile. "Hope you like it here. I certainly do. The Roberts family are such nice people."

"Thank you again, Donna," Gramps said. Then, turning to Cynthia, "Now we'll take a look at the efficiencies if we can find an unoccupied one . . . if not, I can tell you about them. Kate usually takes care of the duties here but it seems Lydia wanted you to know about the whole setup."

After touring the buildings, he took her out to the swimming pool area and from there to the croquet lawn and tennis courts. Every place was busy with activity. Pointing out a huge, two-storied building in the distance beyond the chapel he told her, "That's the new dorm. Have you met Ken Ross?"

"Not personally. I attended chapel last evening and heard him, though. I'm to see him soon and discuss the needs there."

"You want to go today?"

"Not today, thank you. I have off until four o'clock. I'll plan to see him tomorrow. Right now, I think I'll rest outside under those shade trees, it's such a gorgeous day."

"Okay. Remember, I'm here to help you in any way I can. I do hope you'll like it here."

"I already do," Cynthia enthused. "It will take me awhile to get to know about everything, but I like it just fine so far."

"Good. See you around."

After going to the lounge for a couple of magazines, Cynthia went back outside, seating herself fairly near some of the guests, thinking she might learn from listening to them talk if there were any problems. She knew from previous experiences that resort guests often talk these things over with each other.

She heard nothing but good from these particular guests. They talked about spiritual matters mostly. Were all the people here religious fanatics, she wondered!

Promptly at four, after touching up her appearance, she relieved Jason at the office.

"We have a party due in before dinner. Here are their cards with all the information listed. They are regulars, so it will be just routine if they come in before six."

"Okay, Jason, thanks."

"See ya," he called, leaving quickly. "Got a date to play tennis."

"Have fun."

"Oh, I will," he assured her.

Lydia came by just before six to remind her of that evening's get-acquainted activities. "We meet in the main lounge here with the families that are here this week. Ken Ross is in charge. It's at eight o'clock. We'd like to have you join us. Sometimes my daughter Andrea and her family, or my son Jeff and his family, or even both, join us. It would give you an opportunity to meet everyone."

"I'll be there . . . and thanks, Mrs. Roberts."

"We'll dispose of formalities, Cynthia. Please call me Lydia. The younger girls call me Mrs. Roberts," she grinned, "they need that to keep them in line."

"Okay . . . Lydia. Everyone is so friendly here. Where I worked before, everyone just tended to their own affairs. It seems so different and more pleasant."

Don Noble arrived just then to take over the office duties, leaving Cynthia free for the day.

Cynthia attended the meeting in the lounge that evening and came away with mixed feelings. Reliving the events as she brushed her hair, she remembered Gramps' opening prayer and wondered how anyone could talk to God as though he were seated next to him . . . the lively chorus led by Jerry . . . then Mr. Ross asked a member from each family to introduce themselves and add a bit of trivia or a testimony, whichever they desired . . . some had been very humorous, some touching, as they revealed the spiritual changes in their lives —as they walked with the Lord. One family had prepared a skit . . . very light and carefree, bringing forth good-natured laughter . . . yes, it had been a most interesting evening. As she held her brush still for a moment, staring unseeingly into the mirror, she wondered . . . is there only one God . . . Ted had maintained they were made in His image but never that we were answerable to Him . . . these people seemed void of any arrogancy . . . in fact, they appeared humble, not groveling, but as though they were all equal . . . serving one God . . . could it be?

Once again brushing her hair vigorously, she thought, I'll surely find out if I stay here, and I plan to do just that . . .

CHAPTER EIGHT

The following morning, after a leisurely breakfast in the dining room, Cynthia went to the chapel where she had an appointment at 9:00 with Ken Ross to discuss the needs of the teen weeks.

Because she had plenty of time, she sauntered along the way, observing the backdrop of the mountain range in whose foothills the buildings of The Farm nestled. As she followed the paved footpath, she was aware of the velvety lawn enhanced by the gorgeous flowers scattered in attractively arranged beds. She returned Gramps' friendly wave as he passed quite close to the walk on the riding lawn mower. She savored the sweet aroma from the newly-cut grass.

Ken was waiting for her on the chapel steps. "Good morning, Miss Marsh. Lovely day, isn't it?"

"Gorgeous," she replied. "This is a beautiful place."

"I like it," Ken said. "Shall we go to the basement of the dorm, which is the dining room on teen weeks?"

"Oh, so the teens eat separately?"

"Yes. The whole program is a separate thing." He opened the door leading down the stairs into the basement, switching on the lights as he went. "You can see we have plenty of room. This is the kitchen," he explained, opening another door.

Her eyes widened as she took in the modern equipment that revealed careful planning by someone. "Who does the cooking?"

"The different groups bring their own help. Mr. Harrison makes jobs available for each group that have boys who want to come, but can't afford it. I am informed that usually dads or sponsors volunteer for the actual cooking, with boys to run the dishwasher, wait tables, and do the general cleanup after every meal. Mr. Harrison feels that if they want to come badly enough, it will work out. We'll have to see."

"So this is really a pilot venture?"

"Yes, I suppose you could call it that. Mr. Harrison is personally overseeing it. He's a wonderful Christian man." Crossing the room, he opened another door. "Here are the folding tables and chairs we will be using."

"Who does that detail?" Cynthia asked.

"Jerry and I will set them up the day before the boys arrive. Now let's get down to the menu. I believe that is what Mrs. Roberts wants to know specifically about, right?"

"Right. Tell me now, how many guests do you expect?"

"The count is 64, but Mr. Harrison said to plan on a few more."

Taking a notebook from her purse, Cynthia began writing notes. They went back to the kitchen where Ken pulled a chair for her out from a table-desk in one corner and, seating himself beside her, they planned the menus for the week. Cynthia had brought along a menu from the main dining room so they were able to follow that somewhat. When they were finished, she asked, "Will this be the same menu each teen week?"

"More or less, although Mr. Harrison told me that when the inner city kids from Philadelphia come, we'll need to change it some."

"Okay. I'll check with you each week so that Mrs. Roberts can order accordingly. Sounds like a worthwhile project you have going here."

"Of course our main objective is to introduce these teens to the Lord Jesus Christ and to help those who already believe to grow in Him."

Turning aside abruptly, Cynthia said, "If that's all, I must get back. Oh, yes, what about the beds or bunks, or whatever?"

"Mrs. A. takes care of that for us initially, then daily the boys make their own bunks, clean their rooms, and so on. I understand this is part of the conference program for them. Each bunkroom has a counselor. In case of a shortage, Jerry, Jason and I fill in."

"I must leave now," Cynthia said, hardly believing this young man could be so totally committed to this program without being the least bit arrogant. In fact, she came away with the distinct feeling that he felt honored to be a part of the whole thing.

She was glad there was no arrogancy about him. In fact, everyone employed around The Farm seemed to have this same attitude; she hoped no one would disillusion her.

She stopped by the snack bar to pick up Donna's list, going through it briefly with her and asking if everything was okay.

"Would you drop this note into Mr. A.'s box in the office? I have a chair that needs fixing."

"Sure thing," Cynthia replied, waving as she went away.

Entering the front door, she left the note and asked Jason where his grandmother could be located.

"In her office in their living quarters, I expect. She is usually working on books this time of day.

Just go through the hallway from the dining room and rap on the door directly opposite."

The dining room appeared empty now. It usually closed from 10:00 to 11:00 and again from 2:30 to 4:30 in the afternoon, and at 8:30 at night.

Rapping lightly on the Roberts' living room door, Cynthia opened it in response to a distant "Come in."

Lydia appeared in the doorway of her private office. Smiling, she said, "Join me in here, Cynthia. How are things going?"

"Just fine. I had a talk with Mr. Ross this morning, and here is the list of things they need. We tried to keep the menu in line with the main dining room."

"That's good. It'll save time and expense."

"And here's the one from the snack bar," Cynthia handed her boss the paper from Donna.

Taking it from her, Lydia asked, "What do you think of the place thus far?"

"I'm impressed. It all seems to run so smoothly."

"Most of the time it does. Now you said that you served as a social director in your last position. Do you think we need something like arranged tours for some of our older guests?"

"I hadn't thought about it. They all seem very contented. Perhaps one a week. I did notice by the bulletin board that the only service on Thursday is the early morning prayer meeting. Maybe we could plan something for that day. But I'm not familiar enough with the area to make any suggestions."

"Maybe later on." Pausing a moment, she frowned slightly, then said, "I'm rather reluctant to ask this, but would you mind moving into a room in our apartment here for the first week the dorm group comes? It seems at the last minute one of the pastors and his wife decided to join their group and we don't have an extra room. Here, let me show you."

She led the way down the hallway to an adjoining room. Flinging the door open, Lydia said, "This used to be my daughter's room, and some of our other live-in help have occupied it."

"It's a lovely room, Lydia, I wouldn't mind in the least . . . if you're sure I wouldn't be intruding on your family privacy."

"No problem. We rather like having some young life around," Lydia assured her. "I've talked it over with Gramps and it's perfectly agreeable with him. You won't need to move for another week or so. I must get back to work now. See you later."

Cynthia left feeling very welcomed and almost happy.

When she told Matt and Kate about the new arrangement, they quickly assured her that she would still be welcome to visit them anytime, and urged her to still have some of her meals with them. "We will miss you being next door, but we're happy that you are willing to make this change."

"You know, it's a good feeling to be accepted for myself—alone. I've always had this feeling of rejection by people which," she added with a touch of bitterness, "started with my own mother."

Matt said quietly, "There is a promise in God's Word that says, 'When my father and my mother forsake me, then the Lord will take me up.' Jesus never rejects anyone who comes to Him in faith, believing that He died for them to take away their sins. He has promised to never leave nor forsake us."

Cynthia remained silent for a moment before saying, "Uncle Matt, I'm really impressed with the . . . shall I say . . . humbleness of the people around here, but I don't understand your religion enough yet to want to be involved . . ." then impulsively she told them of her near tragedy the night before she arrived at The Farm.

Matt was visibly shaken and told her how he had been awakened that night and prompted to pray for her safety. How he and Kate had prayed and now, he added, "I thank God for answering our prayers.

Cynthia, how horrible it would have been if you had gone into a Christless eternity . . . into everlasting punishment." A tear rolled down his cheek.

Touched by her uncle's caring, Cynthia asked, "Then you believe there is a hell?"

"Oh, yes. The Bible makes it perfectly clear," Matt replied as he reached for his Bible. Turning the pages, he handed it to his niece and said, "Read this."

She took the book a bit reluctantly and read from Luke's gospel about the rich man and Lazarus. She shuddered as she finished. "What is this great gulf that is fixed between man and God?"

"Man's sin is rejecting Christ as his Saviour. Cynthia, dear, why don't you talk with Gramps about this. He is much more knowledgeable than I am about the Bible . . . but this I know, when I accepted Christ as my Saviour, a whole new way of life opened up for me." Taking Kate's hand in his, a rare show of affection for him, he added, "Kate says the same, and it is our constant prayer that you may find the same peace we have through Him."

Cynthia stared at them. They were so sincere, and again she thought . . . humble . . . not even a faint gleam of arrogancy. Her heart was deeply touched by their caring and she promised, "When I move downstairs I'll have a talk with Gramps."

"In the meantime, I hope you'll attend the chapel meetings when you can."

"I'll see . . . I must go now. Thanks again for caring."

She went away with a troubled heart in one sense, but with a good feeling that someone really cared . . . could this Jesus be all they claimed Him to be?

CHAPTER NINE

The following morning Cynthia found it a bit difficult to be up and in the office by six o'clock. A few guests were scurrying along the corridors, which puzzled her for a moment until she saw their Bibles and remembered the early morning prayer meeting.

"Good morning, Don. Hope I'm not late," she greeted the night clerk.

"Right on time, Cynthia, but I must rush. See ya," and he was gone.

He seems like a nice young man, she thought, remembering that Lydia had told her he came from a poor family and had to hold down two jobs in the summer to pay his way through college.

She busied herself going through the guest files to acquaint herself with names and trying to identify faces with them. She noted that nearly all of them were yearly guests.

She was making a list of things she wanted to accomplish that day when the early morning risers started returning. They were trying to be quiet for the guests who were still sleeping. She noted the quiet, happy look on most of the faces and felt a pang of envy. Would this sort of happiness ever be hers?

Later, as she was eating breakfast in the dining room, she overheard two couples seated at the table next to hers.

"That was a very moving prayer meeting this morning, wasn't it?" one lady asked.

"Oh, I think it was just beautiful! Isn't it wonderful to be able to share our problems with others and know they will pray for us!"

"Indeed it is. What a blessing, and did you sense the feeling of unity of the Spirit among us?"

They all seemed to be impressed with the sincerity of the young preacher. As they parted after the meal, one man asked, "Will we see you at the 10:00 o'clock Bible study?"

"We wouldn't dream of missing it," the other couple chorused.

As Cynthia left the room to attend to her daily duties, she thought, they certainly are a religious group of people here. I wonder if they all are trusting this same Jesus Uncle Matt talks about. The thought crossed her mind that perhaps she could find out more by attending the Bible study . . . if time allowed.

As the week progressed, Cynthia found herself liking her job more each day. The guests that stopped by the office or met her somewhere throughout the day seemed very friendly. Each day she was more impressed with the evident inner peace that radiated from nearly all of them. But then, she thought bitterly, they've no doubt all had an easy life . . . still the couple this morning had spoken of problems . . . she shrugged it off and went quietly about her work.

On Friday she worked in the dining room as hostess, which included attending the cash register.

As she was leaving at the end of the morning hours, she encountered a very pretty woman with two chattering children . . . both girls. She approached Cynthia with a smile and an outstretched hand. "Miss Marsh, I'm Andrea Holloway, Lydia's daughter. These two girls are mine, Sara and Becky." The children were very voluble in their greeting as Andrea continued, "We are delighted to have you here. Mom says you are already making her work easier, which is something we have all wanted for a long time."

Cynthia, overwhelmed by the friendly greeting, answered shyly, "I'm enjoying it very much . . . thus far."

"Cynthia . . . may I call you Cynthia? . . . we try to be informal around here . . . I'd like you to meet all of our friends right away . . . it must be lonesome being away from home . . ."

Little does she know about that, Cynthia thought.

" . . . so I'd like to throw a party . . . a lawn party . . . a cookout . . . tomorrow so that you can meet everyone. Would you mind?"

"That's very kind of you . . . but not at all necessary . . ."

Andrea interrupted, laughing, "I love having parties and a good reason makes it all the more enjoyable. Please do say you'll come. I believe you'll like all of our friends."

"That's very thoughtful of you, but . . ."

"Please, Cynthia. I think it would please Matt and Kate, and they are like family to us, you know."

"Okay . . . what time?"

"Early, say 4:30. There is a service at the chapel at eight o'clock. Nearly everyone goes. It's a musical evening, you know. Well, I must go along now and get busy with my phone to round up the gang. Is there anything I can do to help you here?"

"Oh, no, everyone has been most kind."

"Good. See you tomorrow then," and with a friendly smile Andrea was on her way.

After work, Cynthia stopped by her relatives'

apartment hoping to find her Aunt Kate there. Hearing sounds of movement inside, she tapped lightly on the door.

It opened almost immediately. "Why hello, Cindy. Come right in, child. How was your day? Would you like a cold soda? or some iced tea? I'm just having some tea."

"Iced tea sounds good."

"Well, how goes it?" Kate asked again, handing Cynthia a frosted glass.

"Okay . . . I guess. Aunt Kate, Andrea Holloway just invited me to a party at her home tomorrow . . . to meet all of the Roberts' family friends, she said . . . you going?"

"Oh, yes! Your uncle and I are invited. You'll go, won't you? I think it would be good for you to get acquainted with some local people."

"But . . . are they all . . . religious?" Cynthia asked.

"Not religious," Kate replied gently, "but Christians. You'll have a good time. They always have lively parties."

"Can I go with you and Uncle Matt?"

"Of course. We were invited for 4:30. Why don't you meet us here?"

"Okay, I'll do that."

"Now, would you like to eat here with us tonight?"

"I'd love it. I've been in the dining room all day."

Saturday was Cynthia's day off, so she had slept late. Venturing outside in the middle of the morning, she had discovered the swimming pool not in use. Oh, she thought, of course, nearly everyone will be at the Bible study. Returning quickly to her room she changed into her swim suit. Slipping on a terry cloth robe, she hurried back to the pool. As she enjoyed the velvety touch of the water, it was so soothing she felt totally relaxed for the first time in weeks. As soon as she heard the sound of guests returning from the chapel, she hurried back inside.

While eating lunch with her relatives, she asked, "Aunt Kate, what shall I wear this afternoon?"

"One of your pretty matching skirts and blouses will be just fine."

"Okay. I'll see you at 4:30. I believe I'll take my car and drive around this afternoon ... get acquainted with the area."

"I have the afternoon off," Matt said. "Would you like some company?"

"I'd love it," Cynthia responded. "Meet you out by my car in about ten minutes."

"I'll be there."

They spent a couple of hours together while Matt drew her attention to points of interest.

As they sat for a few minutes watching the fiery red gondola ascend the steep mountain so effortlessly, swaying only slightly, Cynthia remarked, "I believe I'll take a ride on that one day soon."

Matt shuddered. "Not for me. I don't really like it, neither does Kate, but you probably would enjoy it. Maybe Jason will go with you one day."

"I'm in no hurry," she smiled at him. "We'd better get back now. I have to wash my hair before we go to the Holloways."

"This has been nice, Cindy," Matt said as they parted back at The Farm. "I do love having you here ... you seem to be more relaxed ... are you really okay?" he asked anxiously.

Throwing her arms around his neck, she gave him a resounding kiss on his cheek. "Thanks to you and Aunt Kate, and the rest of the employees here, I do feel much better. See you in a bit. I'm going with you and Aunt Kate, you know."

"Yup, I know."

Later the three of them walked the short distance down the road from The Farm to the Holloway home, which was just around a bend in the road and not visible from The Farm, Cynthia asked, "Do all of these people know about me? You know . . . Ted and all?"

"No one except the immediate family . . . they had to know because they make all such decisions together."

"Who does 'family' include?" Cynthia asked.

"Andrea and her family, Jeff and his, Lydia and Gramps, that's all."

They were the first to arrive. "We the first ones?" Kate asked.

"Yes, that's the way I planned it. It will be easier for Cynthia to meet the others as they arrive. Cynthia, I want you to meet my husband Greg and son, Robbie." They both greeted her warmly, Robbie saying, "Jase was right! She does have lots of red hair!"

His mother reprimanded him sharply. "Robbie!"

"Well, it's true!" Cynthia laughed.

"And here's my brother and his family. Jeff, Sylvia, this is Cynthia. Cynthia, my brother and his wife, and Anne," indicating the shy 12-year-old, "and Jeffie and Jane."

"We're so happy to meet you," Sylvia's greeting was also warm and sincere.

"Indeed we are," Jeff added. "Mom says you are already a big help to her, which is what we all wanted. She needed to take it much easier."

"It is a big load for one person. I do like it thus far."

Just then Alex, Ellyn and Nathan arrived. "That's Nathan," Andrea laughed as he ran across the lawn to join the other kids.

"Alex, Ellyn, I'd like you to meet Cynthia Marsh, Matt's niece. She's helping Mother, you know."

"So we heard. Welcome to our area, Miss Marsh. I hope you like it as well as we do. Where do you want this tub of soda, Andrea?" he asked.

"Over by the table."

So Alex deposited his load before joining the men.

The women chatted together and finally all the guests had arrived and been introduced; Janelle and Cory Phillips and their three children . . . Janelle's parents, Walter and Flora Stuart . . . Kurt and Lisa Nelson and their two . . . then Jason, Ken Ross, Jerry Thorpe and Gretchen Nelson came; she already knew them.

"I wonder where Reg is," Greg asked, busy at the grill cooking the meat. "If he doesn't come soon, we'll start without him."

Andrea and Sylvia had been busy bringing salads and other food from the house until the picnic table was loaded.

"Everything's ready," Greg informed Andrea. She rang a bell so she could be heard above the children's chatter. They came running at the sound, Robbie shouting, "Oh, boy—food at last!"

"I'll say grace and we'll start without Reg. He must have been held up." As Greg finished praying, a custom which no longer surprised Cynthia, a new voice was heard as a young man appeared. He was of average height, average good looks . . . I guess just an average guy, thought Cynthia, until he spoke . . .

"Hey, what's the big idea! I thought I was invited to partake of this sumptuous feast that I see before me . . . couldn't wait, eh? Where is the guest of honor? That's really what I came for, you know."

"We know," Greg said dryly. "Cynthia, meet Reginald Thomas, better known as Reg . . . bachelor, state senator, real estate and insurance salesman, and in spite of being a little addle-pated, a good friend of the family." Everyone joined in the laughter which ensued, including Reg.

"Hi, Cynthia. They have been hiding you long enough." Placing one hand on his midriff and the other on the small of his back, he bowed low. "Very pleased to meet you, I'm sure. If I collect some of this food, may I sit by you so we can get acquainted? We've wasted enough time."

Feeling her face turn slightly warm, she laughed as she protested, "But I've only been here a week."

"But a week that you haven't known me—totally wasted, in my opinion."

'Oh, no,' she groaned to herself. An arrogant one at last, but he seems nice, and I guess he wouldn't be a friend of this family if he wasn't a Christian.

Reg kept everyone in gales of laughter. Cynthia sensed a feeling of real camaraderie amongst this gathering. She felt sort of a loner . . . inside. Before the evening dispersed, each family invited Cynthia to drop by their home any time, and furthermore, she was always invited when it was their turn to entertain the group.

Later Reg, taking it for granted that she would be attending the chapel service, asked her if he could go along with her. Not waiting for an answer, he called to Matt, "I'll escort your lovely niece to the service, Mr. A."

Pulling her hand lightly through his bended arm, she felt herself going along with him rather willingly.

After the service he insisted on treating her to an ice cream from the snack bar. Leading her to a group of chairs just out of the beam of the lawn lights, he settled her comfortably, handed her the ice cream and said, "Now, let's get acquainted."

"You do come on rather strong, Mr. Thomas," she demurred, although somewhat amused.

"So where do you hail from, Cynthia?"

"A small city in southwestern Pennsylvania."

"How do you happen to be here, might I ask?"

"No, you might not," she responded sharply. "You are getting entirely too personal. I believe I'll go inside now. Please excuse me. Thanks for the treat."

"Aw, don't go away mad. I was only making conversation," Reg pleaded. She hesitated. "Come on," he urged, "you don't want to go inside on this lovely night. Just see that velvety sky splashed so liberally with twinkly stars. Isn't it wonderful of our God to provide us with such a brilliant display of His creation?"

"Mr. Thomas . . ."

"Reg."

"Okay, Reg, you might as well know at the outset . . . I'm not one of you."

He was a bit slow in answering. "You mean, you're not a Christian?"

"Not in the sense that you people interpret Christian."

He answered simply and seriously, "There is only one way to interpret Christian. If one accepts God's Son, Jesus Christ, into one's heart and life as personal Saviour. You see, the Bible tells us, 'There is none other name under heaven given among men whereby we must be saved.'"

"Mr. Thomas . . . Reg, I've just come away from a devastating experience with a so-called religion . . . I'm just not ready for any more at the present."

"Okay . . . sorry. But at least you know where I stand."

"And," she responded firmly, "you know where I stand. It appears to me that all of the 'group' I met tonight have such easy lives, it doesn't take much faith to accept all you say . . ."

"Hey, if you think that, you're dead wrong. There's hardly a one of the 'group', meaning family and friends I assume, that hasn't been through some tragic experiences in their lives. I've been fortunate so far, but . . ."

"Oh, you can't mean Andrea with her devoted husband and lovely family!" Cynthia protested.

"Oh, can't I! Ask her sometime. She's always ready to give her testimony . . . if it's not just out of idle curiosity . . . or Janelle Stuart . . . or Alex and Ellyn Harrison . . . or in a milder sense, Lisa

Nelson—oh, you are so wrong! They would all share their testimony with you any time!"

"You can't be serious!" she asked, aghast. "They all seem so happy."

"That's what knowing Christ as Saviour can do."

"Okay, okay, you've made your point . . . but it's difficult to believe."

"You can believe it," he assured her. "Say," he asked, changing the subject, "how would you like to go bowling and out for pizza Thursday night with our church singles crowd?"

"Another religious meeting?" she asked a bit sarcastically.

"Not really. We meet for a good time together, but we do have a brief time of sharing the Word before we break up for the evening."

"Thanks . . . but no thanks."

"Aw, come on. You'd enjoy our crowd. We do have fun."

"Well . . . I'll think about it. I really must go in now. Nearly everyone has gone."

"Okay . . . good night, and it's been a pleasure meeting you, Cynthia." He grinned impishly. "I've always been partial to redheads. I'll call you the middle of the week about Thursday."

CHAPTER TEN

On Sunday, there was no way Cynthia could avoid going to the chapel services without hurting Uncle Matt's feelings. Both services gave her food for thought. Was it true that everyone was a sinner? Could it be that these people were right? Ken had said in one of the messages that 'The wages of sin is death; but the gift of God is eternal life through Jesus Christ our Lord.' Could it be true that the God these people all seemed to know was a different God from Ted's? How confusing it all was. Would she ever find the answer? Was it really true what Reg had told her on Saturday evening, that nearly all of the friends of the Holloways, including Andrea herself, had had tragic experiences in their lives that brought them to God?

These questions kept burning in Cynthia's mind until, on Tuesday, she went to see Andrea. She had a two-fold purpose for this visit; to find out more about Reg Thomas, and to find out from Andrea herself what Reg had meant. He had said she would share her story with anyone who was not just a curiosity seeker. She had to admit she was curious but she knew that deep inside she really wanted to know what made these people tick ... so different ... so dedicated ... so friendly.

Arriving at the Holloway home around two o'clock, she suddenly felt shy. If Andrea hadn't been outside washing windows she probably would have turned away. But Andrea's cheerful greeting gave her courage again.

"Hi, Cynthia. How nice of you to call. I'll be through here in just a minute, then we'll go to the patio and have cold lemonade." She kept up a friendly chatter while she folded her stepladder and carried it, with her cleaner, around the side of the house. Leaning the ladder against the garage, she said, "Now, then, why don't you get comfortable while I get us a refreshing drink." Her daughters who were playing in the sandbox came running to them.

"Mummy, kin we have a cookie?" Sara asked.

"And I'm thirsty," Becky added.

"Okay, you two, wash the sand off your hands at the faucet ... and be sure to shut it off tightly when you have finished ... and you can join Miss Marsh and Mom here. Excuse me for a minute, Cynthia."

"Of course," Cynthia answered, slightly discouraged ... with the children around, could they talk?

But, after the girls had consumed their snack, they returned to their sandbox to play.

Andrea swamped Cynthia with questions about how the work was going. Then, seeming to sense that Cynthia wanted something, she ventured, "Anything I can do to help?"

Fidgeting around, Cynthia finally said, "Tell me a little about Reginald Thomas, will you? He has asked me to go with him and his singles church group on a bowling party Thursday evening. Should I go? Will it be okay, me not believing the way they do?" She paused and looked anxiously at Andrea.

"You do know about me . . . and Ted . . . don't you?"

"Yes, I know, and am sorry you were treated so badly . . . but it may all turn out for the best, Cynthia. It certainly helped Mom. About Reg . . . he's really a great guy . . . he tends to be flippant and appears to be easygoing, but underneath it all, he is a dedicated Christian . . . a serious senator . . . and a successful businessman . . . not wealthy, but comfortably well off, I'd say. He has the reputation of being a flirt, but my thinking is that he just hasn't found the love of his life yet."

"I'm certainly not looking for any serious involvement myself," was Cynthia's quick response.

"I'd go on Thursday if I were you. You'll like the people you will meet. Just go easy with Reg. Sometimes he gives a new girl a rush for a bit, so just watch it . . ."

"Okay, I guess I'll go. It should be fun to meet some new people. Not that I don't meet them here, but it's not the same . . . being an employee . . ."

"I know," Andrea grinned. "I worked at The Farm all through my teen years after school, and summers and weekends during college. I even help out now in an emergency. It is really a family business."

Cynthia squirmed around, not knowing how to approach the next question on her mind. Finally she blurted out, "Have you always believed in God?"

A wary look crossed Andrea's face. "Why do you ask?"

"Because of something Reg implied to me on Saturday evening after chapel. He spoke about God, and I told him that it seemed to me that all of you people with your secure lives would find it easy to believe. He then told me that nearly every one of your family and close friends had had . . . I believe he used the word tragic . . . experiences before coming to faith in God. He also told me that any of you would be willing to share it with anyone you thought could be helped by it."

"He was right about that, Cynthia, even though it brings back painful memories . . ."

"How much do you know about me . . . and Ted?" Cynthia asked.

"Matt told us you were supposed to be married and he walked out on you."

"Is that all?"

Andrea hesitated. "Not quite all. He said you were mixed up in some . . . religion."

"That's all true. Could I share it with you?"

"Of course," Andrea answered with a smile.

Cynthia then related her past to her new friend . . . from the feeling of rejection by her family . . . which made her vulnerable to Ted Black and his ideas. "I see now that he was so totally wrapped up in his own conceit that he willingly . . . even eagerly . . . embraced the concept that he was a god. Andrea, I could never feel that way about myself, but I did almost worship Ted . . . he was so confident and handsome and strong . . . but, you see, I failed to pass the test of inner strength one needs to feel like God . . . I didn't measure up to Ted's ideals, so he rejected me. I was devastated . . . Andrea, I almost took my life the night before I arrived here . . . then I remembered a sermon I had heard when I visited Uncle Matt five years ago on heaven and hell being very real places . . . Uncle Matt read me a portion in the Bible on hell the other day. Andrea, I'm still confused . . . I don't want to be rejected again . . ."

"But Matt and Kate love you, Cynthia."

"I know . . . or, at least I feel they do . . . and I'm thankful for that; also for your mother and Gramps and your friends, but when they find out about me, will they reject me also?

"Mom and Gramps haven't shown any signs of rejection, have they?"

"No . . . not outwardly."

"If they felt any reservations, you'd know it."

Now, about me . . . it's a long story, and one I'm not proud of, but it does reveal what I went through before I came to know God through His Son. You see, when I was eighteen . . ." Andrea went on to tell her about Jason's father abandoning her before Jason was born, but how her family stuck by her . . . how she had blamed God for allowing her to mess up her life . . . "You know, Gramps was the only Christian in our family for years . . . finally one summer about twelve years ago, first Mom, then Jeff and Sylvia accepted Christ . . . that was the summer Greg came here to recuperate from a viral infection . . . Greg was instrumental in Jeff's conversion . . . then friends of mine came for their annual vacation. Their marriage was on a rocky road, but they came to know God and their marriage was saved . . . somehow I became convicted of my sin . . . you see, I had always felt I had disgraced my family and betrayed myself . . . but that summer I came to the realization that I had sinned against God . . . after I accepted Christ, Greg told me of his love for me . . . we planned to be married . . . then . . ." Andrea's voice faltered.

Cynthia waited patiently, eyeing Andrea as she apparently was wrestling with an inner conflict, " . . . then," Andrea continued in a low tone, "Peter Harrison, Jason's father, appeared and started making claims on Jason . . . I was terrified . . . I won't go into details . . . then Peter was killed in a snowmobile accident . . . then his father Alex Harrison came on the scene and I was frightened anew that he would have some claim on Jason. Alex is extremely wealthy and had been able to buy his way into everything . . . Greg stood by me . . . with the family . . . we finally agreed to let Alex see Jason, but only with Gramps along. To make a long story short . . . Greg adopted Jason . . . Alex continued to see Jason, and by spending time with Gramps, Alex came to Christ . . . that changed his whole life, too . . . until we could finally accept him into our family circle and acknowledge him as Jason's grandfather —so you see how much knowing God through Christ has meant to our family? I can never thank Him enough for forgiving me, then blessing my life with such a godly husband and my children." Andrea looked pale and drawn. "Not a very nice story, is it?"

"And you feel that coming to know God is the basis of all your happiness now?"

"I'm sure of it. Without Him, life would be . . . empty . . . our entire feeling of security is dependent upon His mercy day by day . . ."

"So Mr. Harrison wasn't always what he is today?"

"No . . . as I told you . . . Christ changed his life completely, as He did mine."

"How could you possibly forgive him?"

Just then the girls demanded attention, and Andrea only had time to say, "God's Word says to forgive seventy times seven."

Midst the clamor of Andrea's daughters chattering, Cynthia left after thanking Andrea for sharing her past with her.

"Why don't you talk to Alex and Ellyn some day? Ellyn has a very sad experience to tell . . . and why not talk to Gramps about the deeper things you mentioned?"

"I already promised Uncle Matt I'd do that."

Cynthia walked slowly back to The Farm trying to digest all that Andrea had revealed to her. Was it possible Reg was right about these people; he had certainly been right about Andrea, and who would ever suspect it with the happy life she now had . . . she determined to find a way to talk with Mr. and Mrs. Harrison, and soon. It crossed her mind that perhaps her own problems were insignificant when compared to others . . . but then she wallowed in despair again for a few minutes . . . but it's my life and it all happened to me . . . shoving it from her as best she could, she went to relieve Jason at the office.

That same evening Reg Thomas showed up at the sing-along service, sliding into the seat next to Uncle Matt. Cynthia was seated between her aunt and uncle, so he smiled at her and mouthed the words, "See you later."

The music was good and the songs filled with thought-provoking words about salvation . . . peace with God . . . His sovereign power . . . among others.

Reg managed to get her away from her relatives and once again steered her to the snack bar. Slightly resenting his overbearing manner, she said stiffly, "I only want something cold to drink."

"Okay . . ." to Joan he said, "Two colas, please."

Cynthia sat on a bench near the snack bar with Reg cheerfully taking his place beside her. "Have you decided about Thursday night?"

His attitude of assurance almost tempted her to say no.

"Ken Ross is going to give his testimony. He's had a very rough time in life. Most of the group have not heard it."

"You don't mean to tell me that Ken also has a tragic past?"

"Wait until you hear it! You will come, won't you?"

Intrigued, Cynthia responded, "Yes, I'll come."

"Good. I'll pick you up around seven. We've reserved some alleys for 7:30."

He left soon after that and Cynthia went to her room. Did everyone in the world really have problems . . . well, not everyone, of course . . . somehow, tonight hers seemed to be fading away . . . slightly.

While she brushed her hair, she decided she would start moving her belongings downstairs the next day.

The following two days moved ahead as usual, with Cynthia becoming more used to her work each day. By Thursday, she had everything moved downstairs, to the room she would now occupy in the

89

Roberts' family quarters.

When she informed Lydia that she was going out that evening, Lydia gave her a key to the side door.

Cynthia could see she was curious as to where she would be going, so she told her.

"That's good. Reg is a nice boy, and you'll enjoy the young people."

"Boy? Reg?" Cynthia seemed amused.

Lydia laughed. "He seems like a boy to me, but I guess he isn't. Anyway, I hope you have a nice evening."

"I'm not sure what time I'll be in."

"It won't matter. Gramps and I are sound sleepers. You have to learn to sleep when you can in this business."

"Okay, but I'll be as quiet as possible," Cynthia assured her boss.

After eating supper with her relatives, Cynthia returned to her room to get ready for the evening. She could see they were pleased that she was going with the church group. Indeed, all at once she felt good about it herself as she carefully selected an outfit she thought appropriate to wear.

As she waited for Reg to come for her, she wondered if she would fit in at all. Would this group of people her age be as friendly as the others she had met?

Deciding to meet Reg outside as she had not told him she was moving downstairs, she saw him drive in as she stepped outside the hallway door. He waved to her as he slid out of his car and started toward her. "All set?"

"Yeah, all set," she answered.

CHAPTER ELEVEN

It turned out to be a fun evening, at least to start with. Cynthia was surprised when Joan Fisher showed up with Ken Ross.
"Who's at the snack bar?" she asked Joan, puzzled.
"Donna came back for the rest of the evening. Everything's under control. You with Reg Thomas?"
"Yeah."
"Just watch out," warned Joan with a friendly grin, "he'll break your heart."
"Not mine," Cynthia quipped, "it's immune."
"You like to bowl?" Joan asked.
"Yes, but I'm not very good at it."
"Neither am I," Joan laughed, "but it's fun."
There was much lively banter among the group of fifteen singles. Much give and take in a spirited but friendly manner.
Reg was high scorer, but according to the talk, this was not an unusual thing.
At the Pizza Palace, Cynthia was surprised

when Reg asked Ken to give thanks for the food. In a public place! Where others could hear! She looked around self-consciously during the brief prayer, but no one around them was paying any attention. Really though, she thought, that's a bit much . . . out in public!

They left the Pizza Palace in a hilarious mood, but once they arrived at the church, the mood shifted. Not to one of gloom, but to one of . . . Cynthia couldn't really define it . . . reverence? Perhaps!

One of the girls played the piano while the group sang a few lively choruses . . . still with that sense of . . . what? Commitment? Dedication? Anyway, Cynthia concluded, their attitude contained a subdued sense of inner peace and contentment.

Reg introduced Ken Ross. "Some of you know Ken slightly from attending meetings at The Farm Chapel, but I've asked him to give his testimony tonight. I believe it will inspire and thrill you as it has me."

Ken rose and took his place behind a small podium. Opening his Bible, he said, "I'm going to read only two verses—the first one from John's Gospel, the first chapter. It's a familiar passage but let it renew your thoughts. 'But as many as received him,' meaning Christ, 'to them he gave the power to become the sons of God, even to them that believe on his name'; and now from II Corinthians the fifth chapter, 'Therefore, if any man be in Christ, he is a new creature; old things are passed away; behold all things are become new.'

"So when we accept Christ as our Saviour, God the Father says we are His children, and more than that, we are new creatures in Christ. Life takes on a new meaning and a distinct change of heart. Let me tell you how it changed me." Ken began to tell again of his conversion under Alex Harrison. As he unfolded the events, Cynthia felt a sense of compassion for him. Her life had been void of any demonstrative affection, but at least she had

had a home. When he told of leading his dad to Christ on his death bed, she was near to tears. If she had looked around she would have observed many misty eyes.

He concluded by saying, "I have no idea where my mother is, but I am praying that she will come to Christ in His timing if she's still alive. My testimony is not an unusual one; many have come to a saving knowledge of our Lord under worse circumstances than mine but I praise Him tonight that He allowed these things to happen to me that I might come to know Him. Now the desire of my heart is to serve Him wherever He wants me to."

As he made his way back to his seat beside Joan, Reg strode to the front. In a more serious tone than Cynthia had ever heard him use, he said, "How many of you would like to pray with Ken for his mother?" Cynthia was aware of every hand raised but hers ... she wished the floor would open and she could drop right through it! ... Then she was aware that Reg was praying. What a prayer! She knew she was subtilely being included as one who needed to be saved.

On the ride to The Farm, Cynthia asked Reg about his duties as a state senator. "Oh boy, to answer that in detail would take all night, but I am on a few committees in which I am intensely interested and involved. In fact, I have to go to St. Johnsbury, that's a small city east of here, in a few days for a brief meeting. Would you like to accompany me? You could shop while I attend the meeting, then we could have dinner someplace."

"Sounds like fun."

"Okay, I'll let you know when. By the way, did you enjoy this evening?"

"Yes, very much. They are a very friendly group. I was deeply impressed by Ken's testimony, and Reg ... I talked with Andrea ... she's a terrific person and gives all the credit to God." Wistfully she added, "Somehow I wish I could know this God you all seem committed to."

"You can, you know. All it takes is faith."

"That's all . . . faith? . . . but that's a big order, isn't it?"

Pausing before he answered, Reg said slowly, "Perhaps so for an unbeliever . . . but it seems strange to me now that one could even hesitate."

"Tell me, what led you to believe?" she inquired.

"My conversion isn't nearly as dramatic as Ken's or Andrea's or some of the others, but it is as real. I was brought up in a Christian home, and from the time I can remember, I've heard about God and His Son, but always with the conviction I alone was answerable to God for my own decision. When I was around ten years old, I accepted Christ as my personal Saviour, but it wasn't until I graduated from high school that I committed my life fully to Him."

"So, what were your sins?" she asked almost sarcastically, that you had to be saved from?"

"The original sin that fell upon mankind when Adam and Eve disobeyed God in the Garden of Eden."

"But how in the world could that affect you?"

"Perhaps you had better read the first few chapters in Genesis and then we can discuss it further. Do you have a Bible?" Reg asked, pulling into the parking lot of The Farm.

Cynthia opened her door immediately and slid out saying, "No, I don't have a Bible but I'll get one soon. Good night, and thanks for a pleasant . . . and I must say enlightening, evening."

Reg jumped out and walked with her to the door. "You will go again, won't you? We have an outing every so often. Week after next we're going on a picnic."

I'll think about it."

"I do hope you'll decide to go, and I'll call you before I go to St. Johnsbury, okay?"

"Okay . . . 'night, now."

Once inside, Cynthia found a dim light left

on in the living room. This allowed her to find her way to her room. Moving quietly, she closed her door and rapidly prepared for bed. While brushing her hair, her mind traveled haphazardly back over the events of the evening. *I must get a Bible right away.* Wryly she thought, *it seems as though every night recently while I am performing this ritual, I have some confusing things to think about. Is this what I must do to have peace of mind? Accept this Jesus—but I must know more about it first . . . I don't want to get involved again just on feelings alone.*

The following morning, when Cynthia emerged from her room, Gramps was just leaving the house. "Good morning, Cynthia. I hope you slept well."

"Thank you, I did," she replied, before asking, "Mr. Roberts?"

"Please call me Gramps, everyone else around here does, even the guests," he said with his gentle smile. "I am inclined to look around to see who they are speaking to when I hear someone say Mr. Roberts."

"All right, Gramps. Where is the best place for me to look for a Bible? I need to buy one."

"There is no place near here. We are contemplating opening a Christian bookstore here at The Farm sometime in the future, but how would it be if I loan you a Bible for the time being?"

"Would you? I'd really appreciate that."

Gramps selected one from a bookshelf in the room, explaining, "This is a Pilgrim edition of the King James Version. It has easy-to-follow footnotes. May I ask if you are interested in any particular passage?"

"Reg was telling me about everyone being born with a sinful nature, and advised me to read the first few chapters in Genesis. Where's Genesis?" she asked in a naive fashion.

"The first book in the Bible. Genesis means beginnings. May I ask if you believe in God, Cynthia?"

She stammered, "I—I guess so."

95

With utter simplicity, Gramps said, "If you can believe the first four words in the Bible, you won't have any problem with the rest of it. Here, let me show you." Opening the Bible, he pointed to the scripture, 'In the beginning God . . .' "Now then, as you read study the footnotes, they are very helpful. I would advise you to look up all cross references as you go along. Now I must get to work. We can talk later if you'd like."

"Thank you," Cynthia replied.

After breakfast she went back to her room. This was her day off, so she cleaned her room, then decided to drop a note to her dad. She had promised to write to him and had put it off long enough. After writing a few lines she sealed her envelope and took it out to the office, placing it with the outgoing mail. Don Noble was there. "How goes it, Don?"

"Rather slow today, but it gives me a chance to do some required reading for college. By the way, did Mrs. Roberts tell you that I'm having the afternoon off tomorrow? My mother's family is gathering for a picnic, and I haven't seen some of my relatives since last summer."

"No, she hasn't mentioned it, but I'd be happy to fill in for you."

"I don't know what she has planned. I'm sure if she needs you, she'll ask."

Lydia was in the living room as Cynthia returned to her own room.

"Mrs . . . Lydia, Don just told me you need someone to fill in for him tomorrow afternoon. I'd be more than happy to do so."

"Thanks, Cynthia. I was going to ask you. Gramps and I are meeting with Andrea and Jeff to discuss business of The Farm.   Sure you don't mind?"

"Not in the least. I'm more than happy to be of use wherever I can."

"Okay. I'll see to it that you get some extra time off when you want it."

Sunday afternoon turned out to be quite busy. Several guests checked out and a few parties checked in. Later in the afternoon Lydia came to the office. "I have another request, Cynthia. We decided this afternoon that it would be less confusing for the teens if we have them check in at the dorm. That means someone has to be there. Jason offered, so if you could stay on here until he gets through, I would appreciate it. I would like to be around this first morning. The file on the guest listing for the dorm is separate so there won't be any mixup on that score."

"I'd be happy to do that for you, but who will take care of the duties I've been doing?" Cynthia asked.

"I thought Gramps could relieve you here around ten for an hour or so. There's not much we can do about the menu over there, at this late date, anyway. The bunks are all made up . . . Kate has assured me that all is ready in the dorm. But I'd still like to be around to welcome the leaders. I do pray this venture will be a spiritually successful one. Alex so has his heart set on helping teens in this uncertain world. He and Ken make a great team. It is my understanding that Alex sent out booklets on "Temptation for teens in this present world . . . and the answers from God's Word." Each guest is supposed to have read it and be ready for discussion. By the way, the schedule will remain the same for this week. Alex and Ken decided that Ken would hold the teen Bible class early, then the accompanying counselors will take over, with Jerry to help while Ken has the adult class, as usual. I do hope Ken won't be overdoing it."

"Sounds like a full schedule," Cynthia agreed. "How about Thursday meetings?"

"We will only have the regular prayer meeting. Ken has Bible study with the boys, then he'll have the rest of the day off. By the way, we have a men's brass ensemble coming for Saturday night from a midwestern Bible college. They will have the entire service, so Ken will be relieved that evening."

"I haven't seen the names on the weekly guest list, have I?"

"No," Lydia replied. "The Harrisons have invited them to stay in their home. See you later. Don should be back soon to relieve you here."

Cynthia watched the bustling little woman leave, saying to herself, Where does she get all of that energy!

Monday was rather a hectic day. Jason didn't get through until two o'clock because one of the buses broke down and another driver had to return for the guests.

Cynthia was really tired and only too ready to go to her room where she showered and dropped down on her bed for a nap, thinking that now time off to go with Reg to St. Johnsbury should not be a problem. Before sleep captured her, she thought fleetingly—I mustn't get to liking Reg too much . . . I'm just not ready for that . . . or am I? But what good would it do? She'd been warned about him . . . although, thus far, he had shown no signs of anything but friendship toward her . . . oh, well, as her mother always said, "Take life as it comes."

CHAPTER TWELVE

Reg Thomas called Cynthia early Tuesday evening. "I'm sorry I can't get over to the meeting tonight but I'm tied up. I'm leaving for St. Johnsbury tomorrow at 2:00 o'clock. Can you get away for the rest of the day?"

"I'm sure I can," Cynthia replied, "I've been working overtime the last two days."

"I'll pick you up at two, then."

"I'll have to check with my boss before I can make final plans."

"Just call me if you can't go, okay?"

"Give me your number," she paused to jot it down. "If you don't hear from me, I'll be ready."

Cynthia attended the meeting with Matt and Kate that night and listened carefully to the lyrics of the music. They were all centered around God and His holiness and His prominent part in the life of a believer. She promised herself that very soon she would make time to read the passage in the Bible that Reg and now Gramps had suggested.

Having obtained Lydia's approval about the afternoon off, she was waiting for Reg when he drove in promptly at two o'clock.

He settled her comfortably on the front seat of his car and they were on their way.

"Have any difficulty getting the time off?" he asked with a friendly smile.

"No. As I told you, I've been putting in some overtime. Besides, the Roberts are very good to their help," Cynthia responded.

"So I've heard. You like it here then?"

"Love it."

The conversation drifted from one subject to another during the drive, with Reg pointing out places of interest. He detoured briefly in Montpelier to show her the capitol building where he spent his time during the legislative session which was usually from January to the end of April, with committees meeting now and then the rest of the year.

Arriving in St. Johnsbury, he parked his car in front of the building where he was to meet his colleagues.

"I'll only be half an hour or so. You can take my car and drive around if you like," he said as he got out.

"I think I'll just windowshop," she replied.

"Okay, see you soon." With a wave of his hand he opened the door of the brick building and disappeared.

Cynthia took her time getting out. She wandered along the street until she came to a ladies' clothing store. After viewing the window displays she went inside, deciding on impulse to look for a divided skirt for the picnic. That seemed to be the accepted style among most of the girls, although a few wore slacks.

With a saleslady helping her, she found a lime green divided skirt with a matching blouse which fitted perfectly. She decided to buy them.

Looking at her wristwatch as she left the shop,

she went back to the car, for it was nearly time for Reg to be through with his meeting. She was barely settled when he appeared.

"You have just been sitting here?" he asked.

"Oh, no, I went shopping."

"Look," he said, "one of the fellows gave me these brochures and told me this was an interesting place to visit."

Scanning the paper Reg handed her, Cynthia read, "Maple Grove Maple Museum and Factory. Sounds interesting."

"It's only a short distance. Want to take it in? We have time before dinner."

"Sounds like fun. Yes, I'd like to, if you would," Cynthia agreed.

"Okay, we're on our way." He took a sharp right and in no time drove into the parking lot beside a brick building boasting a huge sign, 'Maple Grove,' above the stairs leading to the entrance door.

"Here we are," he announced unnecessarily.

"So I see," Cynthia grinned.

Once inside, Reg paid the modest fee and they were soon watching the enchanting process of maple syrup being boiled to the right temperature to be poured into huge vats where it was stirred by large beaters into a delicious-looking concoction which was, in turn, poured into molds on a revolving counter. Nuts were added to some of the vats whose contents would be made into fudge. It was all fascinating to watch. They also went downstairs to where the candies were being packaged into attractive boxes ready for the gift shop.

Leaving the building, they walked along a flower-bordered walk to the Maple Museum where they watched the sap being boiled down, ready for candy processing.

"It says here that it takes 35 to 40 gallons of sap to make one gallon of syrup," Cynthia remarked.

"I've never really paid much attention to the maple sugar industry, though it is one of Vermont's oldest and proudest business traditions."

"It also states that this is the Maple Center of the World."

"Yup. Guess it is at that," he agreed. "Want to go to the gift shop?"

"Of course," she answered. "I wouldn't want to miss that."

Once inside, they made the rounds of the displays, with Cynthia selecting a few items to be shipped to her father. "He's got a sweet tooth," she explained to Reg.

"Guess I'll get a gallon of syrup for my folks. I heard Mother say the other day that she was nearly out." Their purchases accomplished, Reg said, "Now for the movie."

But the attendant said, "Sorry, the final showing for the day is just winding down."

At Cynthia's look of dismay, Reg said, "Never mind, we'll come again some day, or better still, I'll take you to a rural sugar house next spring when they will be in full operation. I haven't visited one since I was a kid and it's time I did. Now, is it too early to eat?"

"Not for me. This delicious aroma has caused my appetite to work overtime," she laughed. "Besides, we have a long drive ahead of us."

"So we do," he grinned.

They went to a restaurant in town which had attractively arrayed tables, with pristine white tablecloths and an extensive menu. It was early, not many diners there yet, so they were waited on promptly.

The meal was delicious and the service excellent. They lingered over their coffee and dessert until Cynthia noticed the waitress was glancing at them with an anxious look, and suddenly realized the restaurant was filled with people.

"I think we had better leave, Reg. The place seems to be filling up and no doubt they need our table."

"Right you are," he answered. "Let's go then,

shall we?" Leaving a generous tip, Reg paid the bill and escorted Cynthia to the car.

They chatted amiably on the way home about trivial matters. As they turned into The Farm entrance, Cynthia exclaimed, "Look at the star-splashed sky. Isn't it gorgeous?"

"The heavens declare the glory of God," Reg murmured reverently.

Once again Cynthia had the distinct feeling that these people knew a personal God that she herself was unaware of, but a brief sense of yearning to know this God herself suddenly overwhelmed her. "Reg," she asked, "can anyone know this God you worship?"

As he walked with her to the door, her package under his arm, he answered, "Why of course one can. 'For God so loved the world that he gave his only begotten Son, that whosoever believeth in him should not perish but have everlasting life,'" he quoted. "It's that simple, Cynthia. If you really want to know Him, the bottom line is to believe that Jesus died for you, shed His blood on the cross for you, was buried, rose the third day, and now is seated at the right hand of God where He ever liveth to make intercession for us—that is, those who know Him as Saviour."

"You make it sound so easy and simple, Reg."

"It is. But one must be sincere about it all . . . believe with the heart, not just the head."

They arrived at the door, and Cynthia reached for her package. "Good night, Reg, and thanks for a lovely day," she said.

"It was my pleasure, Cynthia . . . you will think over what we have just talked about, won't you?" he seriously entreated.

"Yes, I'll think about it," she answered as she slipped through the door, repeating again softly, "Good night."

"See you soon," he replied gently.

Lydia was in the living room relaxing with

the daily paper when Cynthia walked in.

"Hi, Cindy," her boss greeted with a smile. "Have a nice day?"

"Super! We went to the Maple Sugar Factory. I mailed some goodies home to Dad. Then we had dinner and," she added, "I bought a new outfit." Drawing the box from a shopping bag she displayed her new clothes.

"Um, nice. Good color for you."

"I'm going to hang these up before I go back outside for a bit. It's a beautiful night."

Lydia, returning to her paper, replied, "Good idea. Stay as long as you like, Cindy."

There were several young people still around the snack bar. Locating a chair outside the limelight she watched with amusement Jerry Thorp and Gretchen Nelson together as usual, and Jason with a new girl. There seemed to be a different one each week or two and Jason sheepishly admitted that his attitude toward girls had changed, but as he told Cynthia that morning, "Not the silly ones—I'll leave that kind to someone else." These four appeared to be having a good time together, tossing lighthearted banter between them, occasionally bursting out with a line or two of a chorus.

Cynthia's heart saddened within her as she thought of what it must be like to grow up in a Christian home. This thought evoked the old feeling of bitterness toward her mother and Ted. Wearily she went inside, directly to her room. Crawling into bed, she tossed and turned with mixed emotions gripping her. She somehow knew that she could never know peace with this God and harbor feelings of bitterness . . . what was it Andrea had said . . . Jesus said forgive seventy times seventy . . . but how could one do that? Finally she fell into a troubled sleep from sheer mental exhaustion.

Friday night Cynthia once again attended the chapel meeting. That night Ken Ross spoke from John's Gospel on 'Do The Work Of God.'

He read, "Then said they unto him, what shall we do, that we might work the works of God? Jesus answered and said unto them, this is the work of God, that ye believe on him whom he hath sent."

Ken then expounded unto them the gospel once again. "The very first thing a person must do is believe on the Lord Jesus Christ as his or her personal Saviour."

Then from Hebrews he read, "But without faith it is impossible to please him; for he that cometh to God must believe that he is, and that he is a rewarder of them that diligently seek him."

Cynthia was listening intently as she thought once again that Ken's God and Ted's were so different; certainly not the same one. She sort of liked the idea that Ken's God was one that would take one's cares and burdens; furthermore, it seemed that there was more difference than that. Once again she sensed that Ken's God was to be worshiped while Ted's God was to worship himself. She couldn't quite fathom it all yet, but she was feeling herself drawn to the God these people worshiped.

Ken ended by saying, "If anyone here doesn't know God the Father through Jesus the Son, remember this, God's grace is everything for nothing to those who don't deserve anything. Furthermore, it seems to me that any thinking person would choose God's grace rather than face God's wrath, for you know, beloved, that one day at the name of Jesus every knee shall bow to the glory of God the Father."

As the congregation sang, 'What can wash away my sin, nothing but the blood of Jesus,' Cynthia felt like responding, but she couldn't quite bring herself to do so; she must have time to understand more thoroughly what it all meant . . . but this decision left her with a vague emptiness, a feeling which was not very pleasant.

Saturday was Cynthia's day off, and after a morning spent leisurely shampooing her hair, plucking her eyebrows and fixing her nails, she had a light lunch and returned to her room determined to read the scripture pointed out to her by Reg.

After taking the Bible from her bureau, she seated herself comfortably in one of the easy chairs, and with trembling fingers opened it to the book of Genesis.

As Gramps had suggested, she read the introduction first. As she read about the beginnings of everything: the world, man, sin, civilization, agriculture, music, poetry, and so forth, she became intrigued. Then when she read about Lucifer, the fallen angel—reading the reference also—who is now known as Satan or the Devil, she was a bit bewildered.

When she started the text itself it certainly seemed believable—she remembered what Gramps had told her—if she could believe the first four words, 'In the beginning, God'—she wouldn't have any trouble believing the rest. Somehow in this atmosphere it was easier to believe, or to try to.

Avidly she read about the creation, and when she came to verse 26 of the first chapter, it hit her full force. "And God said, let us make man in our image, after our likeness" ... then verse 27 ... "So God created man in his own image, in the image of God created he him, male and female created he them."

Entirely absorbed, she read on ... there it was in chapter three, where the devil tempted Eve. When she came to the part where the serpent said, "For God doth know that in the day ye eat thereof, then your eyes shall be opened, and ye shall be as gods, knowing good and evil."

Having read the footnotes regarding the serpent ... and how he was cast out of heaven by trying to be equal with God, she gained a glimpse of the false religion Ted had led her into ... with unusual perception she thought, this religion of Ted's, wanting to be as God, is no new thing. It would appear to me that it started way back here in the beginning.

As she read about Adam and Eve's excuses when God sought them out, the question fluttered through her mind, why would they disobey God when they had it so good? As she pondered the consequences of what a heading in the Bible called 'The Fall of Man,' she decided she needed to talk with someone. She decided to see if Gramps was around.

Keeping her finger on her place in the Bible, she went in search of him. He was in the pantry getting a cold drink. "Oh, here you are," she exclaimed. "Do you have time to talk with me for a few minutes?"

Seeing the Bible in her hand, he said, "Certainly. I'll be right with you. Will you wait in the living room?"

When he reappeared, he had a scrubbed, relaxed look, and in his gentle tone he asked, "Now, how can I help you?"

"I've just been reading about the creation and the fall of man. First of all, I do believe in God now and that He created everything, but a few things puzzle me."

"Okay, tell me and I'll help if I can."

"First of all, why would God allow Adam and Eve to sin?"

"Well, you see, God made man with feelings, emotions, a will of his own, and so on. I always believed that God wanted man to worship Him because he chose to—not from force. So in a sense I believe God allowed this to happen because He made man with a free will. But, you have to remember that then, as today, the devil can be very persuasive and somehow he can make wrong seem right. There are many things we do not know, but one thing we do know is that God did not leave man in his sinful condition without a way out. In the Old Testament, He instituted the sacrifices that required the blood of a perfect animal to cover the sins of all who believed. Then, as you have heard Ken preach, He sent His Son, Jesus, who knew no sin but became sin for us that we might be made the righteousness of God in Him."

"So when He made people in His image, He wanted them to worship Him because he is God and not to be like Him or equal, as Lucifer tried to be?" Cynthia quizzed.

"Exactly," Gramps replied sincerely.

"Do you have time to listen to my experience with what the leader called a New Age religion?"

"Certainly. Tell me."

So Cynthia related to him about Ted and his beliefs, and how she had been drawn into it, but quickly added she never could believe she could be a god. Ted had no problem with that, though," she stated pensively, "he is so arrogant and filled with self-confidence."

"But don't you see, child, this is no New Age movement. Lucifer told the same old lie to Eve in the garden that he's telling today, and sad to say, many people are believing it, and it appears that Ted is one of them."

Sighing heavily, Cynthia said slowly, "I'd like to know God as you people do. To have the peace and assurance you have." Then she told him of how she had almost taken her life on the way to Vermont.

Thoughtfully, Gramps said, "We were all praying for you, you know. We didn't know what your problem was, but we knew you had one. God mercifully spared your life. Won't you accept His Son, Jesus, as your Saviour now? It's the only way to peace for you."

As she sat there, a look of despair crossed her face as she said tragically, "I can't—I just can't! There's something in my life God wouldn't like."

"There is no sin big enough that God won't forgive, if you truly repent and ask Him to."

Jumping up from her chair, she mourned, "But it's something I've lived with for years inside me—

and I'm not even sure I want to let it go. So, I just —can't."

"But, Cynthia . . ." Gramps urged.

Rushing toward her bedroom, still clutching the Bible to her, she cried out, "No . . . not now. I just can't."

Gramps' sorrowful look followed her and he dropped to his knees and prayed that God would comfort Cynthia and remove the barrier that seemed unbearable to her, that she might have His peace.

Later, Lydia tapped lightly on Cynthia's door and reminded her of the concert at the chapel.

Answering through the closed door, Cynthia said, "Guess I'll pass it up. I'm tired tonight."

"Okay, Cindy, see you in the morning."

CHAPTER THIRTEEN

Cynthia wished afterward that she had gone. Walking around her room like a caged animal, she could hear the brass instruments in the distance, and they sounded wonderful.

Toward morning, she fell into a restless sleep, and was still sleeping when her phone rang at nine o'clock. It was Lydia.

"Cindy, I'm in a bind. Gramps has come down with a cold. Jason has plans for the afternoon, and Don would like to be off from 12:30 to 6:00. Would you mind taking over? It will be busy as we have several parties checking out and some coming in."

"I'd be happy to help out," Cynthia answered.

"Fine. Thanks, Cindy."

It was a busy afternoon, for which Cynthia was grateful. It gave her no time to think. After Don returned, she had a light supper in the dining room before deciding to visit her relatives.

"Hi, Cindy. We've missed you. Come in, come in," Uncle Matt invited. "I understand you had to work today."

"Yes, but I didn't mind," she replied. "I wonder how Gramps' cold is."

"I saw Lydia when I went down for our supper," Kate said, "and she seemed worried. He has a slight fever tonight. She said if he isn't better in the morning she plans to take him to the doctor. Seems strange. The rest of us catch things, but **Gramps**—almost never."

"Are you going to chapel tonight, Cindy?" Matt asked.

"I think not. I'm bushed, and I have early morning duty tomorrow."

It turned out to be a hectic week. The following morning around seven, Lydia came rushing into the office. "Gramps is no better. Has a fever, so I'm taking him to the doctor if I can get him in and," she continued, "Jason is needed to mow the grass today. You know Gramps does a section each day to keep it looking neat . . . Jerry will take over the registration at the dorm for the new group . . . and of all mornings, one of the maids called in sick . . . Andrea is going to take her place, so if you will stay on here until Jason gets through with the lawn . . . he can only work on it so long because of the guests milling around . . . well, I must be going . . . oh, yes, I'll tell Donna and Ken to bring you their lists if I'm not back by ten . . . then will you order for me? . . . the numbers to call are on my desk in the other office . . . I don't know what I'd do without you, Cindy."

"Don't worry about a thing, Lydia. We'll handle it. Just take care of Gramps."

"Thanks, dear," Lydia answered as she hurried down the corridor.

Cynthia was accustomed to quick changes in the hotel business, so these minor problems presented no difficulty for her.

Lydia and Gramps didn't return from the doctor until nearly noon. The ordering had been done, the lawn mowed . . . everything was going well.

"He's got bronchitis," Lydia reported. "Bed rest, lots of liquids, and an antibiotic. Cindy, can you take over our duties at the desk as I have to stay with him, and, oh yes, Jason will be needed to mow every morning, probably the rest of this week, although he should be through by 8:30 each day. I'll make it up to you somehow."

"Not to worry," Cynthia responded, "that's what I'm here for."

When Reg came Wednesday night for the chapel service, Cynthia wasn't there, so he went to her after the meeting to inquire about the picnic the next day.

"I'm sorry, but I'm afraid I can't go," she told him. "We're so busy here, I'm bushed by evening."

She thought he showed a momentary disappointment, but he only said, "I understand. Maybe next time."

Thursday, Cynthia received a short letter from her father thanking her for the maple products. He said he was enjoying them very much. He was happy that she had arrived safely and liked the job. Things were the same at home, although he missed her very much and urged her to write again soon. He wanted her to say hi to Matt and Kate for him. Not a word about her mother, oh well, what did she expect anyway . . .

By Saturday Gramps was much better and able to sit up for awhile each day, but Lydia asked Cynthia if she would be willing to continue the present schedule for another week. "Gramps has been so ill, I want him to have a complete week of rest before he begins his duties again. I wish he would let me hire a man to take over for him, but he refuses to consider it."

"He's a very giving, caring person, isn't he?" Cynthia remarked.

"Indeed he is. Our whole family is very, very fond of Gramps."

"And from what I have observed, many of the guests are, as well."

Lydia agreed with her.

Cynthia was really bushed by Friday night, so she slept later than usual Saturday morning since it was her day off. When she finally decided to get up, she dressed quickly and, snatching the sheets from her bed, she went up the back stairs to the laundry room for clean ones. Kate was there and greeted her warmly.

"Why don't you have lunch with us today, Cindy? We have missed seeing you this week."

"I'd love to, Aunt Kate. What time?"

"Around 12:30, is that okay?"

"Sure thing. I got up so late I skipped breakfast."

Scurrying back to her room she made the bed up fresh, cleaned her bathroom and went out to the hall closet for the vacuum.

Gramps was in the living room and called to her. Vacuum in hand, she paused in the living room door. "Hi, Gramps, feeling better?" she inquired with concern.

"Much better. I hope to be back on the job next week. I feel like a slacker."

"You shouldn't; from what I understand, you're almost always working."

"For which I am thankful, considering my age."

"Pooh," Cynthia smiled, "you'll never be old, Gramps."

"Why thanks, child."

"I have to finish cleaning my room now, then I'm having lunch with Uncle and Aunt."

As she turned away he asked gently, "Have you been thinking any more about our last conversation?"

A troubled look creased her brow as she answered, "Almost constantly." Turning away abruptly, she mumbled, "I must get busy."

Vacuuming furiously, she tried to drown out her thoughts, and almost succeeded.

Later, lunching with her relatives, she told them she had heard from her father and everything was the same at home.

Matt and Kate both had to be back at work so she didn't stay long. As she was leaving Matt inquired, "Going to the chapel meeting tonight, Cindy?"

"I think not," she answered quickly. "I'm still tired from such a busy week."

"Tomorrow?" Matt asked, trying not to be too eager.

Cynthia, however, sensed his eagerness and agreed, "Tomorrow I'll be there . . . for the church service, anyway."

"Did you know we have a family musical group coming Tuesday for the rest of the week?" Kate asked.

"Yes, I've seen it on the guest list. They will be staying in one of the efficiencies, although the son will be at the dorm."

"They have an outstanding reputation, both as performers and in their Christian testimony."

Once again sensing these two who seemed to care deeply for her would be hurt if she didn't attend some of the meetings, she said casually, "I plan to take in some of the sessions."

The beaming looks that came her way made her happy to please them.

"I have to get back to work," Matt declared.

"And I do, too," Kate said with a sigh.

"Aunt Kate, don't you feel the responsibility you have here is too much for you?"

"Lydia thinks so, Cindy. In fact, she is on the lookout for the right person to assist me."

"I hope she finds someone soon. Right now, I have to finish cleaning my room, then I think I'll go for a walk."

"See you tomorrow then," Kate said as they parted outside the door.

Turning to the back entrance, Cynthia spied a piece of paper leaning against the hall baseboard.

"Litterbug," she grumbled, stooping to pick it up. As she started to crumple it, she noticed the red lettering—'does everyone need love.' Muttering to herself, "You'd better believe it," she stuffed the paper into her pocket to read later, but when she reached her room, she pulled it from her pocket, dropped onto the edge of the bed, and opened it up.

'We all need love, children,'—"and how," she muttered to herself—'all ages, even the elderly. But do we all have it? No, we don't. There is so much indifference toward each other—even within the family circle. And,' she read on, 'of course the devil is the instigator of the hatred, jealousy and evil deeds done toward those that should love each other, but instead often even hate them.

'BUT, God is love. In I John 4:8,9 we read, He that loveth not knoweth not God; for God is love. In this was manifested the love of God toward us, because that God sent his only begotten Son into the world, that we might live through him.'

This made her think of the verse Reg quoted to her about God sending His Son into the world that whosoever believeth in him should have . . . what was it he said? . . . everlasting life.

She read on. 'God wants us to love others as He loves us. Once we are a child of His through accepting Jesus as our Saviour, we are commanded to love each other.'

Crumpling the paper, she sat with anger seething through her entire body. How could she possibly love and forgive her mother . . . she had already forgiven Ted, and even felt grateful that she had escaped from his influence . . . or could it possibly have been God's intervention because of Uncle Matt's and Aunt Kate's prayers?

Springing to her feet, she threw the paper into her wastebasket and turned to her work. Soon she stooped to retrieve it, smoothed it out, and placed it between the pages of her Bible. She'd read it again later when she had calmed down.

Around three o'clock, work done, showered, shampooed and dressed in her new lime green outfit, she started her walk. Heading toward the main highway, she relaxed in the shade of the stately maple tree branches overhanging the road, while a slight breeze fanned the leaves. She slowed down from her fast pace, listening to the melody of a variety of birds. It all had a soothing effect.

As she approached the younger Roberts' residence, Andrea Holloway and her girls were just emerging from the driveway, headed home. Becky was in a stroller with Sara hanging onto the side of the handle.

"Hi, Cynthia, out for a walk?" Andrea greeted with a smile.

"Yes, and it's so relaxing."

"We have had a busy two weeks, haven't we? But, thank the Lord, Gramps is much better so things should be back to normal next week."

"I was glad to help out, and I noticed you were there on several occasions, too."

"I often help when I'm needed in different places. Listen, why not walk back with me and have supper with us? I'm trying a new dish. Reg is coming, and he and Greg will be planning an activity for a church group of boys, so you could keep me company while they talk. I think these girls are going to be ready for an early night. Robbie is staying with Jeffie overnight, so how about it? I'd love to have you. It would be a change for you, too."

Cynthia protested, "But I'm practically a stranger . . . and I wouldn't want Reg to think I was . . . was . . ." she felt her face grow warm as her voice faltered.

"Chasing him," Andrea laughed. "I'll explain to him that I begged you to come to keep me company, okay?"

"Well . . . if you think it's okay . . . I do have some matters I'd like to discuss with you."

"Perfect timing, then."

So the two of them visited companionably during the walk back to the Holloway home.

Becky was quite fussy so Cynthia held her while she watched Andrea fix the kabobs.

"Mmm, that looks yummy," she remarked as Andrea placed layers of chicken breast, chunks of pineapple, shrimp and pieces of sweet red papers on skewers.

"These have been marinating in a soy and lime juice mixture. Now they're ready for the broiler. Next I need to mix the sauce."

Placing the ingredients, consisting of chicken broth, peanut butter, coconut, garlic and other ingredients, in a saucepan, Andrea remarked as she put it on a burner to thicken, "I sure hope this is good. I'm always a bit leery about using a recipe of this nature as Greg is usually a strictly meat-and-potato man."

"Sure looks good to me," Cynthia enthused.

"There, that's done," Andrea remarked. "I think I'll give the girls their baths and an early supper. Becky is about to fall asleep and Sara will get cross if she gets too tired. I'll only be a few minutes. Why don't you relax in the living room with a magazine?"

"Don't worry about me, Andrea. It was so nice of you to invite me to stay. It's a pleasant change for me."

Andrea smiled. "It's nice for me, too—remember."

Once the girls were bathed and fed, Becky was indeed ready for bed, while Sara crept onto the sofa. "She will probably go to sleep there but she doesn't like to go to bed without seeing her daddy first. She's missed him all afternoon. He doesn't as a rule work on Saturday, but it was the only time he could get depositions for a case he's involved in. He should be along any minute. We invited Reg for 6:30. I do hope Greg won't be late."

He wasn't. He arrived just a few minutes later.

Greeting his wife with a kiss, he said hello to Cynthia stating he was glad to see her, and announced he was headed for the shower.

"Sara is waiting for you in the living room, Greg, for you to tuck her in bed for the night."

"Okay, will do," he answered.

"Reg should be here soon, so I'll pop these kabobs under the broiler. We'll eat on the patio, it's so pleasant out."

"Anything I can do to help?" Cynthia inquired.

"Not yet. You can help me put it on the table when it's all ready."

Reg arrived on schedule, seeming surprised but pleased to see Cynthia there.

The meal was served simply without any fanfare, and was declared by everyone, even Greg, to be delicious. Andrea had served rolls with crispy crusts and insides as light and puffy as a gentle summer breeze. The conversation was genial with much happy laughter, as though the group enjoyed being together.

After Greg and Reg withdrew to discuss the business they had, Cynthia helped Andrea clean up from the meal.

Andrea took a peek at the girls before they settled comfortably in the living room with the ceiling fan making the air pleasantly cool. "You mentioned you would like to talk with me about something?" Andrea smiled.

"Yes . . ." Cynthia suddenly felt shy, "but . . ."

"Just go ahead," Andrea urged.

Cynthia unknowingly clasped her hands together, entwining her fingers so tightly that her knuckles were white. "It's just that . . . Andrea, how could you possibly have forgiven Jason's father for deserting you . . . and Alex, when you were afraid he was trying to take Jason from you?"

Pondering a moment before she answered, Andrea said, "I couldn't until I had given my life to Christ."

"But you blamed God for your problems . . . didn't you?"

"For a long time—yes, I did, but when I saw myself as God saw me, a sinner in need of a Saviour, I knew I needed His forgiveness—I shall never cease to be so thankful for that. It was only when I yielded to the Spirit's control that I could . . . forgive. It could be that way for you, too, Cynthia."

Cynthia spoke slowly. "I have certainly learned a lot since I've been here. I have observed and felt the caring attitude of the entire Roberts family . . . as for Uncle Matt and Aunt Kate . . . they are super."

"They do care for you deeply," Andrea assured her.

"I'm so afraid of being rejected again . . ." Cynthia quietly cried out, "and I can't seem to let go of the bitterness I feel toward my mother."

"And Ted?"

"Oh . . . Ted . . . I've long ago forgotten him . . . he's so mixed up about the things of God."

"Just let go and let God handle it all," Andrea urged.

The distress Cynthia felt showed in her face and actions. "I can't . . . just yet."

"It took me a long time, too, Cynthia. Don't force it, it'll come when you are ready, and I believe it will be soon now."

"Do you really?" Cynthia asked with eagerness.

"It would appear that way . . . but your own will is involved, you know. I know from experience that the longer you hold out, the more miserable you will be. Now then, let's talk about something else . . . but remember, we're all here for you anytime if and when we're needed."

Cynthia relaxed somewhat as Andrea talked about everyday matters. Finally Andrea exclaimed a bit impatiently, "I wonder what is keeping those men so long? I thought they would be through by now and we could play a game of Pictionary."

"You know, Andrea, everyone is wrong about Reg being a flirt . . . or it could be me . . . perhaps it is me . . . he is so friendly and courteous . . . I have yet to see the Reg everyone warned me about."

"You could be right, Cynthia. I have sometimes thought that myself. Underneath Reg's lighthearted appearance and bantering words, he is really a very dedicated Christian." Eyeing Cynthia with a strange look, she said, "I wonder . . ." Just then the men appeared, and Andrea cried, "What have you been doing? You've had time to settle the problems of the entire world."

"Well . . . perhaps we have," Reg drawled laughingly.

"Let's play Pictionary, shall we?" Andrea asked eagerly.

As they played, Cynthia relaxed little by little until she, too, entered into the fun.

Later, as she rode the short distance to The Farm with Reg, he asked her if she would be interested in attending a barbecue with the singles group at his home the following Thursday.

"If I can get away, I'd love to."

"Okay, see you then. Tonight was fun, wasn't it?"

"I enjoyed myself immensely. Andrea and Greg are a nice couple, aren't they?"

"The best," he agreed as he left her at the door. "I'll pick you up Thursday at six then, okay?"

"Okay. If I get tied up, I'll let you know." She watched him disappear into the night, whistling softly.

CHAPTER FOURTEEN

The following morning Cynthia slid reluctantly onto a seat beside her Uncle Matt in the chapel. If she hadn't promised to come she would have stayed away. It seemed as though she was confused enough about religion now. She felt she needed to assimilate what she already knew, and how it all really affected her before she could take in more; therefore, she resolved to turn off her mind to everything Ken said today. But she found that didn't work at all because Jerry sang, "You Cannot Hide From God," during which she squirmed inwardly while trying to maintain outward composure. Then—halfway through his message, Ken paused—the kind of pause that focuses everyone's attention on the speaker.
"I've been talking about the love of God, but I would be neglecting my duty if I did not warn you once again about the wrath of God. Oh, I know some people ask how a loving God could send anyone to hell, but as I've told you before, and I repeat —He has left the choice up to us . . . if we reject

His offer of salvation . . . of becoming a child of His through His Son Jesus, we are responsible for our own lost condition. God is not willing that any should perish but that all should come to repentance. My friend, if you do not know the Saviour today, won't you ask Him to save you now . . . right now. You know, every time you hear the gospel and you turn away from it, your heart becomes a little harder and it becomes easier each time to reject Him, until you no longer feel the need . . . I know those are harsh words I have spoken, but beloved, sometimes it takes harsh words spoken lovingly to stimulate action of the will . . ."

Cynthia once again turned her mind off, quivering inwardly—just what does he know about my heart—my problems—then she was filled with a sense of confusion again as she remembered Ken's background . . . how could he so easily forgive his mother for deserting him and now be concerned about her . . .

Not fully conscious of the fact that it was still her own stubborn will holding her back from the peace her yearning heart desired, Cynthia avoided Ken's searching gaze as she shook hands with him at the door.

She walked back to the motel with her relatives, dreading the lonely afternoon ahead of her . . . she talked incessantly until Matt's voice finally penetrated. "Cindy, do you want to go?"

She stared blankly at him. "Go? Where?"

"As I said, for a ride, and then Sylvia called this morning and asked us to stop by later today and wanted us to bring you, too, if you'd come. They would like to get better acquainted with you. How about it?"

"I'd love to, Uncle Matt." Anything to get away from her thoughts.

"Why don't we all eat in the dining room today?" Kate asked. "Then we can leave directly after dinner."

"Sounds okay to me," Cynthia agreed.

Later that afternoon on the way back from their ride, Matt pulled his car into Jeff's driveway.

"Well, it's about time!" Sylvia called from the side door. "Jeff is out back freezing some homemade ice cream. The Holloways are here, too. Make yourselves at home while I get some dishes for the ice cream."

Sylvia dashed off with her usual quick movements. In no time they were consuming fresh banana ice cream and fluffy chiffon cake. The amiable conversation was varied and interesting as they talked about world and local affairs. Aside from the prayer before the meal religion was not mentioned, which surprised Cynthia . . . still, there was a certain atmosphere which prevailed that made Cynthia sense the importance of Christ in their lives.

She excused herself from chapel service that evening explaining that she had to be on duty at six the next morning.

Her duties and lunch behind her at 12:45 on Monday, Cynthia decided to take her car and explore the countryside for herself.

A few miles down the road she spied an interesting-looking narrow road lined with trees on both sides. Impulsively she turned onto it, not noticing the sign which read, 'PRIVATE—DEAD END.' After about two miles she found herself in front of a remodeled farmhouse. With dismay, she discovered the only way out was to drive close to the garage and back out. Just as she neared the building, a young woman stepped out of the side door. A look of recognition crossed her face as she lifted a hand in welcome and called, "Hi, Cynthia. How nice of you to stop by."

Cynthia felt trapped. It was Janelle Stuart, Andrea's friend.

"I'm sorry, I got lost and was only trying to turn. I didn't mean to intrude," Cynthia apologized.

"Intrude? Nonsense. Now that you are here, please come in. I'd love to have you."

Cynthia hesitated, then she remembered that Janelle was one of the people Reg had mentioned who had a tragic past. Perhaps this was a good time to find out. "Okay, I'll stop for a few minutes, but I still feel I'm intruding."

Janelle laughed and, sliding her arm through Cynthia's, she led the way to the side door which opened into the kitchen.

"What a lovely room," Cynthia enthused.

"It is, isn't it? I love it myself, but," her hostess remarked, continuing on, "this is where we practically live in the summer, especially afternoons when we are in the shade."

"How very cozy," Cynthia exclaimed, viewing with appreciation the attractively arranged white wicker furniture with matching tables on the large glass-enclosed porch.

Janelle's two girls, Tricia and Bede, were playing dolls at one end of the room. "Say hello to Miss Marsh, girls."

"Hi, Miss Marsh," Tricia dutifully said.

"Hi, Miss Marsh," Bede echoed. "Would you like to play dolls with us? I'll share."

Cynthia laughed softly. "Thank you so much, but I think I'll just visit with your mother this time."

She listened for a few minutes while the girls seriously discussed a change of clothing for their 'children,' and whether or not to have a tea party.

Tricia called out, "Mom, can we have a tea party?"

"Sure thing, honey. Miss Marsh and I will have one, too, okay, Cynthia?"

"Sounds like fun."

After the girls were settled with their miniature tea set and cookies, Cynthia found herself comfortably seated in a wicker chair with a tray on her lap, facing a very friendly hostess.

"This is nice," Janelle remarked smiling. "Tell me, how do you like it at The Farm? I loved it when I worked there."

"Very much," Cynthia answered. "The Roberts are such nice people."

"The best," Janelle agreed. "The way they took me in as a childhood friend of Sylvia's was fantastic. I am originally from California. I understand you are from Pennsylvania, and Matt Anderson is your uncle, right?"

"Right," Cynthia answered, wondering how she could get Janelle to tell her about why she came to Vermont, when her hostess casually remarked, "It's strange . . . and yet it isn't . . . how many people with needs . . . all kinds . . . turn up on the Roberts' doorstep. I well remember," she continued, "when I arrived at Clarissa Fields' home after my cross-country drive, how quickly Sylvia landed me a job at The Farm."

"You mentioned Sylvia as a childhood friend. Was that in California?"

"Yes, we lived on the same street, and although Sylvia was a bit older, we were friends."

"Janelle . . . could I ask you a personal question? You see, I am having a difficult time making an important decision. I mentioned to Reg Thomas one night that all of you people seemed so secure, it would be easy to trust Christ as your Saviour. He very candidly told me that several, including you, have had tragic experiences in your past. Andrea told me hers . . . she was lucky though, see how she turned out?"

"I'm sure she wouldn't call it luck, Cynthia. She would call it God's graciousness to her, the same as I do. I'll tell you how I came to be in Vermont but I'll only mention the high spots."

"If you'd rather not . . ." Cynthia said.

"Not if you feel it might help you. First of all, did you come to your Uncle Matt's seeking spiritual help?"

"I think down deep I was, but not consciously."

"Okay, briefly, my mother had been dead for only a year when my father decided to marry Flora.

She was impossible at that time and I couldn't bear the thought of her taking my mother's place. I decided to marry a man who worked for my father, to escape. I didn't love him, but it seemed at the time to be a sensible solution. Then I discovered that he was being unfaithful to me, so I headed for Vermont. Clarissa Fields had been a close friend of my mother's—my mother came to know Christ a few months before she died and afterwards I discovered a letter from Clarissa in my mother's Bible. I didn't believe in God then so I came to the Fields' knowing they knew Him, and I wanted to find out if He was real. Then, after talking with Gramps, I soon became a Christian. After a visit from my father and Flora . . . I'm leaving out a lot of details . . . I discovered Flora was okay after all and good for my father, and also was on my side as far as maintaining my independence. Of course, all of this did not happen overnight. When I married Cory, my father was not at all pleased. My father is very wealthy, you know, and couldn't understand my willingness to marry a laboring man." Janelle chuckled. "It still amazes me how Flora manages my father and he isn't even aware of it."

Bewildered, Cynthia asked, "But I thought your parents were Christians?"

"Yes, they are. Flora came to know Christ first and then Father, through Alex Harrison's witness. At first he couldn't understand a man with Alex's wealth—Alex is extremely wealthy, also—needing or wanting religion. But Alex's consistent testimony finally convinced my father of his need, for which I am grateful. My mother's prayers for both of us have been answered."

"How could you forgive your father for the way he hurt you, if I understood correctly."

"It wasn't easy, nor quickly, but after becoming a Christian, I finally realized that I must forgive also, to be entirely at peace."

Just then a wail from Bede split the air. Janelle

jumped to her feet and rushed to her side.

"Tricia hit me, and it hurts," she screamed.

"Did you hit her?" Janelle demanded of her older daughter.

"She wouldn't mind me and I'm the play mother," Tricia answered sullenly.

"You know the rule is no hitting. Now you go to your room at once."

Glancing at a clock on the wall, Cynthia gasped, "Oh no, it's 3:30! I must rush. I'll be late for work. I have to be on duty at 4:00 o'clock. Thanks so much for a wonderful afternoon and for sharing this with me."

"I only hope it helps. Someday I'd like to hear about the decision you need to make, if you want to share it."

"I do," Cynthia responded grimly, "but I must rush now. Thanks again, Janelle."

As she drove the speed limit back to The Farm, Cynthia tried to piece together Janelle's story. Evidently she had been hurt badly enough to leave home, too. Maybe it would all work out for her, too, in time . . .

She was busy from four until Don Noble arrived at six to take over.

The Miller singing group arrived Tuesday morning and were assigned one of the efficiency apartments. Cynthia decided to skip that evening's service, feeling she was too unsettled to get anything from it anyway.

However, the following day she heard such glowing reports of their performance that she decided to attend that evening.

As she sat by Kate, she was intrigued by the versatility of the group. It seemed all of them could sing any part in an ensemble group or by themselves. The son played the guitar, the mother the piano, while the father played both violin and trombone. They were very good.

When the mother rose to give her testimony,

Cynthia froze in her seat as the leading question was, "Have you ever felt completely rejected?" Her first thought was, how dare someone tell her about me. Then she relaxed a bit as the speaker said, "Of course, I know nothing about any of you personally, but I'd like to tell you about my conversion to Christ."

Cynthia was so uptight that she only caught pieces of what was said . . . "Parents were archaeologists . . . traveling all over the world . . . sometimes she could accompany them . . . sometimes not . . . when not, she was left with a very strict maiden aunt who knew nothing about the emotional needs of a child . . . or an adolescent . . . or a teenager . . . she felt so good when her mother would write a letter and send a gift . . . until she found out that her secretary did both . . . she grew up feeling unloved . . . rejected . . . when she was eighteen her aunt died and she went to college . . . got in with the wrong crowd until she met Bill Miller . . . she immediately fell in love with him . . . he seemed attracted to her and she couldn't understand his standoffish attitude until one day he told her he was a Christian. Really! she thought, does that make any difference? Little by little he had drawn her life story from her and then told her of the One who would never leave her nor forsake her . . . she held out until she received word of an airplane crash in a far-off country and learned that both her parents were killed . . . this caused deeper bitterness as she realized how unimportant she had been in their private lives . . . they had left enough money for her to finish college . . . in the meantime, Bill took her to church and she had accepted Christ as Saviour. As she grew in Him, she was healed from all bitterness and finally came to the conclusion that "all things work together for good to them that love God." Now she could thank Him for the past tragic events in her life and she had promised to serve him always."

Cynthia, unable to stand any more, excused herself saying she had a headache which, indeed, she did. Once outside she made her way quickly to her room where she flung herself across her bed, her whole body trembling violently. Could it be that if she accepted Christ He would take away the bitterness of rejection from her—this terrible feeling toward her mother . . . somehow, she no longer wanted to hang onto it, to feel this way.

After what seemed hours to Cynthia, she found herself on her knees beside her bed crying out to God. "Oh, God, if You will forgive me my sins and make me a child of Yours, I promise I'll serve You in any way I can, although as You know, I do not have many talents but I do believe Your Son Jesus died on the cross for me. I want to have the peace I sense in the people around me."

Gradually, as she knelt, she grew calmer until her whole being was permeated with the peace she was searching for. "Thank you, God, for hearing me. Now, if You will help me get rid of the bitterness toward my mother . . ." and as she continued to kneel, she sensed the feeling of bitterness slipping away, and she remembered Andrea's words, "Forgive seventy times seventy."

"Okay, Lord, I'll try . . . if You will help me."

Much later, slipping into bed, she fell into the most peaceful sleep she had experienced for a long time. There was even a trace of a smile upon her lips . . . a relaxed, happy smile that had not been there since she was a small child.

CHAPTER FIFTEEN

When Cynthia awoke the next morning she felt so totally relaxed that she was bewildered for a moment, then with a surge of joy she remembered, "Thank you, Lord, for accepting me into Your family." While lying there, she couldn't seem to bring to life any feeling at all toward her mother—"Help me, Lord, to not only get rid of those horrible feelings, but to really love her . . . and Oliver . . ."

Reaching eagerly for her Bible, she opened it at random and began to read. She had opened to the book of Proverbs. As she read, a feeling of wanting to know God better encompassed her. 'Trust in the Lord with all thine heart; and lean not unto thine own understanding. In all thy ways acknowledge him, and he shall direct thy paths.' Pausing there, she prayed, "Help me to know Your will for my life. I truly want to serve You."

Bounding happily from bed, she found herself humming snatches of the hymns she had heard lately. This feeling of happiness permeated her being and she prayed that she could retain it always.

Emerging from her room, headed for the dining room, she was surprised to find Lydia and Gramps seated at the table in the family room. They were usually busy elsewhere this time of day.

Blithely she said, "Good morning to both of you."

She sounded so happy that they both gazed at her wonderingly. With quick perception, Gramps asked with a deep questioning look in his eyes, "Cynthia?"

Radiant but suddenly shy, she remained mute, nodding her answer. Lydia, quickly sizing up the situation correctly, exclaimed, "Cynthia, how wonderful!" Reaching her arms out, she hugged her close and placed a gentle kiss on her forehead. Cynthia noticed a trace of tears in her eyes as well as in Gramps' as he took both of her hands in his, saying, "Welcome to the family of God, Cynthia. Now you are truly one of us. When?"

"Last night by myself and oh, Gramps, Lydia, I'm so relieved and happy, and the peace I have cannot be described."

Gramps murmured, "The peace of God which passeth all understanding."

Breaking away, Cynthia said, "I must tell Uncle Matt and Aunt Kate."

"They will be absolutely thrilled, my dear," said Gramps. "I think you'll find Matt in his workshop."

"I'll run out and speak to him right now and then find Aunt Kate. I think I have time before work."

Lydia beamed. "Take as much time as you need, dear."

Sure enough, Matt was in his workshop. Surprised, he greeted her, "Good morning, Cindy, anything wrong?"

"Everything is finally all right, Uncle Matt."

Hopefully he looked at her. "You mean . . ."

"Yes, Uncle Matt. I accepted Christ as my

Saviour last night. I was so under conviction that I ran away from the meeting, but I couldn't run from God any longer." Throwing her arms around his neck, she kissed him on the cheek. "I'll never be able to thank you and Aunt Kate for praying for me and making it possible for me to come here."

"Does Kate know yet?"

"No, Lydia and Gramps were in the family room, and when they saw me . . . they just knew. Now, I must hurry and tell Aunt Kate or I'll be late for work. I'll see you at lunch time . . . and thanks again, Uncle Matt."

"If you only knew how happy this makes me, Cindy."

"I think I do," she said.

After she found Kate and told her, receiving the same loving response as Uncle Matt had given, Cynthia grabbed some toast and coffee from the kitchen and began her day's duties. Oh, what a difference in her attitude! She could understand now the enthusiasm that motivated her co-workers in their dedicated service to God. She herself now rejoiced to be one of them at last.

As she got ready for the outing at the Thomas home that evening, she was filled with a sense of exuberance tinged with a bit of shyness. How would she tell Reg . . . and Joan . . . and Ken? "Help me, Lord, as I tell them about my new relationship with you."

At a quarter to six her phone rang. It was Reg. "Hi, Cynthia. I'm sorry, but I'm running a bit late today. Dad needs me here. I've asked Ken to bring you along with him and Joan, do you mind?"

"Of course not," she assured him, not completely understanding or acknowledging the fact that she was disappointed, besides why should she be? Right now she'd better hurry as she didn't want to hold Ken up.

Ken and Joan were as friendly as ever but Cynthia was keenly aware of a difference in their attitude toward each other. It seemed to her that they were hardly aware of her!

When they arrived at the Thomas home, Cynthia was astounded. On a rise, the building loomed like a small castle. Surrounded by a well-manicured lawn and stately elms, the white house trimmed with black shutters, small-paned windows, cupolas, a turret extending several feet from the high two-storied building seemed austere and impressive to her. Ken drove around the house and parked in a paved lot that would have done justice to a country inn.

Reg was waiting and immediately opened the car door to help Cynthia out, apologizing again for not coming for her, but in his lighthearted manner exclaimed, "But you'll find the chicken worth it. Dad prides himself on his barbecued chicken and I might add, rightly so."

As they walked the short distance to the building, Reg looked at her. "You seem different tonight, Cynthia . . ." Stopping in his tracks, he stared wide-eyed at her. "Have you . . ." he faltered as she shyly nodded. "Well, praise the Lord! Tell me about it."

"Later," she smiled radiantly as he opened the door to a screened and glassed-in patio, built onto the house but still appearing to be a part of it. Nearly everyone was there and they were all welcomed warmly by the elder Thomases.

Mrs. Thomas greeted Cynthia by saying, "You will have to wait to meet my husband later. He'll be like a bear if we interrupt him now. Make yourself at home. I understand you know all of the group. Excuse me, please," she said as Mr. Thomas called,

"Lucy, the chicken is ready."

Cynthia was impressed with the room. She had seen nothing like this in her life. Along one wall was a built-in barbecue gas unit about ten feet in length, cased in with white brick. Two sides of the room were opened to a view of an emerald green lawn and a beautiful weeping willow tree beside a narrow winding brook. Patio doors the height of the room were opened to the screened section. This gave one the illusion of being outside. It all blended together for an enchanting atmosphere, with comfortable chairs attractively placed, inviting relaxation. A long table had been placed in the center of the room so the guests, which numbered only twelve tonight, could all be together during the meal.

Baskets of all descriptions adorned the back wall, some with flowers, others merely ornamental. Along the back wall a table was laden with food. She observed all of this briefly.

Reg, leaving the barbecue, asked Ken to pray, and as he did so, Cynthia felt a new kinship, no longer on the outside. She could now be included with the others in the sincerity of a thankful heart for God's blessings.

After the prayer, Mrs. Thomas invited everyone to help themselves to the buffet supper. When it came her turn, Cynthia found Reg directly behind her. As she picked up a plate with divided sections, she remarked, "I've never seen anything like this. They are ceramic, aren't they?"

"Mother had them made especially for occasions such as this."

As she heaped the plate with the enticing food, starting with the chilled fruit cup, salads, vegetables and dip, hot Italian bread which had been buttered and sprinkled with garlic salt, topped off with the barbecued chicken, she laughed. "All of a sudden I feel ravenous."

"It would appear that we all are by the looks of our plates. Let's join the others, shall we?"

As Reg seated her at the table she noticed that Ken and Joan were seated a bit apart from the others. Turning to Reg she asked, "Think there's anything serious between Ken and Joan?"

"It would seem that way, wouldn't it? They began seeing each other last year but I have noticed them together more often this summer."

A pleasant time ensued, as comparative quietness

prevailed until the appetites were satisfied. They all complimented Mr. Thomas on the chicken while some who knew him quite well teased him for the sauce recipe he used, knowing full well he would never give it away.

"Come on now, I've worked for years perfecting this recipe, and I don't intend to give it away," jokingly adding, "unless I leave it to Ken in my will."

Mr. Thomas was such a young-looking man, appearing in excellent health, they all moaned in mock dismay, "Then you'll just have to be our caterer in the meantime."

Mrs. Thomas was about to serve dessert, but the girls declared they were too full to hold another mouthful. Reg suggested they have the dessert later. Everyone readily agreed.

Reg then asked how many would like to pitch horseshoes. After a time of good-natured badinage, all of the men and two of the girls made up two teams of four each, leaving the other four for the cheering section. Cynthia, in the cheering section, thought to herself, Christians do have fun, and such good, clean fun . . .

At dusk they went back inside. Mr. and Mrs. Thomas had removed all traces of the meal, except the table which had been cleared for dessert.

"Who's for dessert?" Reg inquired. "It's brownies with ice cream and chocolate sauce."

Everyone seemed ready for it now. "Coming right up," he said. "Ken, how about some help?"

The two men returned soon with trays bearing the dessert. It was dark by now but with the soft wall lights the room appeared even more attractive.

Reg closed some of the sliding glass doors against the chill of the evening air before he announced, "We have no special speaker for tonight. I thought we could share as we feel led of how the Lord has worked in our lives recently."

One after another gave testimony of God's goodness to them, even though some of it came through trials.

Reg then asked if any had prayer requests. A few were forthcoming, and he asked Ken if there was any update about his mother's whereabouts.

"No," Ken answered, "but Alex Harrison has a detective working on it."

Cynthia had been tense during the testimony time, wanting to tell them about her conversion, but somehow felt reluctant to speak out. Reg had cast questioning looks her way, and she knew he was giving her an opportunity to tell them about it.

Quite suddenly, surprising even herself, she began speaking, gaining courage as she went along. The group listened with apparent compassion as she let it all come out . . . about Ted and the false religion she had been involved in . . . the feelings of rejection at home . . . the peace she now had since accepting Jesus as her Saviour just last night. "This is all so new to me. Will you all please pray for me that I might grow in the Lord and become all He wants me to be."

Ken spoke, "I know I haven't been asked to speak tonight, but Cynthia's testimony about this New Age religion should cause us all to be concerned. I have been reading more about this lately, and even many Christians are getting drawn into certain phases of this cult by false representation. There is, of course, nothing wrong with trying to improve oneself . . . but the danger here is that for a Christian it must be the result of allowing the Spirit to guide us . . . not in trying to go it alone . . . and sad to say this is what is being taught . . . you can be all you want to be if you only have self-confidence . . . but, my friends, our only confidence must be in, as the song goes, 'my only confidence is in Jesus' name.' Many people say they believe in God . . . but how they define Him and think about Him is something else . . . there are a couple of verses in Romans the first chapter that say, 'Because that, when they knew God, they glorified him not as God, neither were thankful; but became vain in their imaginations, and their foolish heart was darkened. Professing themselves to be wise, they became fools.' In other words, they claim to be made in the image of God, as this man Cynthia mentioned, but do not believe He is sovereign. So let's beware lest we be drawn into a trap that promises to raise our self-esteem, make us more competitive in our field of work, or such enticements in the wrong way. I didn't intend to speak tonight, but I felt prompted to do so."

"Thank you, Ken, for sharing your thoughts with us. Now, shall we have a time of prayer, with all taking part who feel led to do so."

The prayers that followed were brief but to the point and touching in their sincerity.

At the close of the prayer time, the girls gathered around Cynthia, embracing her and showing their happiness in her conversion. The men followed, shaking her hand and assuring her she had just made the most important decision of her life. All of this strengthened her inner peace and happiness.

She was preparing to leave with Ken and Joan when Reg asked her to please wait. He would like to drive her home. Thinking that this would allow Ken and Joan more time alone together, she agreed.

Their hosts appeared once again to bid everyone good night, and as Cynthia approached them, Mrs. Thomas smiled and said, "My dear, I hope you will forgive us, but we were sitting in the next room and heard your testimony. We are so pleased for you. I do hope we see you again soon."

"Yes, indeed," Mr. Thomas beamed, "we do love having young people around us."

Reg then said, "I'm ready, Cindy. Good night, Mother, Dad, and thanks."

They left with Mr. Thomas' words ringing in their ears, "Anytime, son, anytime."

Most of the drive home was made in silence.

Cynthia felt happier than she had in years. As they turned onto the road leading to The Farm, Reg asked, "This man . . . Ted, did you call him? . . . were you in love with him?"

She was thankful for the darkness that hid her hot face as she stammered, "I thought I was . . . but, Reg, how could it have been real love when now I only feel pity for him, and am so thankful I was spared from marriage to him. Just think what I would have missed . . . no, Reg, I'll never believe it was real love . . . why do you ask?"

"Just curious. I'm so happy that now you are one of us. I've been praying for you ever since the night you so vehemently informed me that you weren't a Christian."

"Thank you, Reg. I guess many people have been praying for me, and how grateful I am that God cares and that He hears and answers prayer."

As he left her at the door he said, "Would you like to go out for dinner with me Saturday evening and then come back here for the concert?"

"I'd like that very much," she answered with a lilt in her voice.

"Okay, I'll pick you at five so we'll have plenty of time. 'Night, now."

"'Night, Reg. I had a wonderful time tonight."

"I'm glad—see ya."

Her heart was almost bursting with joy as she went to her room, humming happily to herself.

CHAPTER SIXTEEN

The following morning Cynthia was almost late at the office, arriving just a minute or two before six.

"Good morning, Cynthia," Don greeted her with his usual cheerful manner. "Thought you were going to be late, for sure. How was the barbecue last night? I sure hate to miss these outings but I have to earn the money for my education and I am grateful for this extra job, even though it really does tie me down."

"We had a super time! Mr. and Mrs. Thomas are such gracious hosts."

"And Reg?" he grinned.

"Of course," she retorted.

"'Bye now. See you this evening."

"Have a good day, Don," she called after him.

Finding things slow this morning, Cynthia decided to write her parents to share with them her latest news. She grabbed a sheet of paper and a pen but felt her confidence dwindle as she stared at the blank paper in front of her. How do I start? How should I break the news? She knew her dad would be happy for her but, no doubt, her mother would be indifferent. Feeling a momentary resentment against her mother, she remembered what Ken had said the night before, "Our only confidence is in Jesus." Closing her eyes she prayed earnestly for the Lord to guide her in writing this letter. After her prayer, the words flowed freely from her thoughts to the paper.

"Dear Dad and Mother, I am writing to tell you that I have accepted Jesus Christ as my Saviour. I have discovered that Uncle Matt's way is the only real way to God. I am happier than I have ever been in my life!

"Also, I wanted you to know that I am grateful that our family has managed to stay together even though the way has been rough at times.

"Dad, I wish we could have had the conversation we had the morning I left to come here, many years ago and, Mother, even though we have never been close . . . and now I wonder how much of it really was my fault . . . I want to thank you for all you have done for me. Tell Oliver about my new life and tell him also that he is missing out on the most important part of this life, if he doesn't yield to God. I am enjoying my work here and expect to like it even more now."

Nibbling at her pen, she thought, can I really sign it 'with love'? Is my love for them sincere? I truly want it to be. Finally she decided it would be honest to sign it 'affectionately, Cindy.' "There, that's done," she remarked aloud. Sealing and stamping it, she placed it with the outgoing mail and breathed a prayer that her family would try to understand.

She had a busy day, as the following week the inner city teens were due at the dorm. This meant a longer talk with Ken regarding the menu. He had received correspondence from the head counsellor of the group and it seemed that these kids would require a different menu. Most of them came from families on the poverty level and were not accustomed to eating regularly. The letter contained suggestions for meals . . . the two of them decided to make up a menu for the first two days and see how it went.

"I'm not sure I'll get my regular day off next week," Ken said, "but that's okay. I'm looking forward to the challenge."

"Have any of these kids ever been to a camp before?" Cynthia inquired.

"I don't think so, but Alex knows the leader of the mission in Philly and between them, they made these plans. Confidentially, I think Alex is paying most of the expenses. It would be like him."

"You think a great deal of him, don't you?"

"Sure do. To me, he is the same as Paul was to Timothy . . . sort of like I'm his son in the faith." Changing the subject he asked her, "How's the new life going?"

"Great, Ken. I've never been so happy, but I do have a problem."

"Can I help? I've a few minutes more to spare."

Briefly explaining her life at home, she ended by saying, "I truly want to change this relationship. I don't think it will be hard with Dad, but my mother and Oliver, I just don't know." She also told him about the letter she wrote.

"That sounds like a good start. Seems like all you can do now is pray about it and wait until you get an answer, that should show you how to deal with the situation. There are many places in the Bible that show us how God wants us to love others. I would suggest that for now, you read the third chapter of Colossians. We've been studying that book in our morning Bible study. If you like, I'll even loan you a study book."

"I would appreciate that, Ken."

"I'm due at the chapel soon, so I'll walk along with you and get a copy now if you want."

Handing the book to her a couple of minutes later, he offered, "If you have any questions, I'll try to help you, or Gramps will, I'm sure. The Lord bless you, Cynthia, in your new life in Him."

"Thank you, Ken. I really feel like a new person. See you later, and thanks again for the book."

She met some of the guests arriving for the morning study session and wished she had time to remain, but she had a job to do and she must get to it.

* * * * * * *

Cynthia slept late on Saturday. After taking a few minutes for Bible reading and prayer she cleaned her room, finishing just in time to lunch with her relatives.

"Uncle Matt, I wrote to Dad and Mother about my conversion. What do you think they'll say?"

Rubbing his chin in a thoughtful gesture, Matt answered, "I wouldn't dare guess what your mother might say, she had nothing but disgust for Kate and me. But your dad will be pleased, I'm sure. Guess you'll just have to wait and see."

They both beamed at her the whole time she was with them.

"I'm having dinner with Reginald Thomas tonight, then we are returning here for the Miller concert. I'm really looking forward to that. You know, it was Mrs. Miller's testimony that really broke me up."

Matt nodded. "I thought so."

"I told the gang at the Thomases Thursday night and they all seemed pleased. I'll see you tomorrow . . . at Sunday school . . ." she grinned. "Now I have to get ready for my date."

On her way downstairs to her room, she thought happily, this is my first real date with Reg . . . and then her heartbeat quickened as she thought with astonishment, and I'm really looking forward to it . . . also acknowledging to herself . . . I could really like that guy . . . better go easy. Still, she retained that excited feeling all afternoon as she made special efforts with her grooming . . . finally selecting a pleated white skirt with a summery white sweater splashed with sequins, and white shoes with ankle straps.

Styling her hair, she gazed at her reflection critically. One beautician had called her hair 'sun bronze,' and had remarked about her dark brows and lashes making a most unusual contrast. Using light makeup, as usual, she finally had to be content. Reg remarked at their first meeting that he had always been partial to redheads . . . one thing was sure, his friends were all wrong about him . . . he was not a light-hearted flirt . . . or, at least he hadn't treated her in that manner . . . was it possible that he wasn't attracted to her at all . . . but why else would he invite her out for dinner . . . oh, well, she would enjoy the evening, anyway.

Finally ready, she bowed her head and closed her eyes for a moment of prayer. "Lord, protect me from being hurt again . . . I no longer feel rejected because I belong to You now . . . but I don't want to be hurt again . . ."

Reg arrived promptly at five. Escorting Cynthia to his car, he said, "You look lovely tonight. Just right for the place where we are dining."

He was dressed in a suit she hadn't seen before, a dark pinstripe with a perfect fit. "You look pretty spiffy yourself," she assured him.

He took her to a place in Burlington that wasn't much to look at on the outside, but was quite elegant on the inside. Even a maitre'd who seemed to know Reg.

"Your table is ready, Senator Thomas," he said, leading them to a secluded alcove. "The yellow corsage for the lady is beside her plate. Your meal will be ready shortly."

"Thank you, Mitch," Reg smiled.

Cynthia was glad she had worn a pretty outfit. "These flowers are beautiful, thank you." She smiled shyly at Reg while she pinned the corsage to the shoulder of her sweater. "These yellow roses are gorgeous, just gorgeous . . ."

"I ordered our main meal when I made the reservations. Shall we visit the salad bar now?"

"Sounds great to me," she answered, rising to follow him. "Oh, so much to choose from," Cynthia's eyes shone, "and I am starved."

She selected a serving of shrimp cocktail and a few crackers, with Reg following her example. "Better take the green salad to go with the prime rib."

"You choose for me," she begged. So he followed her back to their table with a loaded tray. Their assigned waitress was at their table, filling their glasses with ice water.

"Coffee now, Senator?"

"Later," he told her.

"My name is Marie. Please let me know if there is anything I can do to make your dinner more enjoyable."

"Thank you, Marie, we'll do that," Reg assured her with a smile.

Before they ate, Reg reached across the table, clasping one of Cynthia's hands in his and asked God's blessing on their evening. Instead of being embarrassed, Cynthia glowed with pleasure, thinking, Reg has really accepted me as one of them.

It was a most satisfying interlude for Cynthia. Their conversation was congenial and the soft background music from an invisible violinist made for a perfect setting.

At six-thirty, Reg declared, "I hate to break up the delightful time, but we'll be late for the concert if we don't leave now . . . or could we skip it tonight?"

"I'd rather not. I want to hear the Millers again. You know, it was her testimony that convinced me of the need of Christ in my life."

"Then let's go," he replied.

The concert was wonderful and so inspiring. The whole group sang as the closing number, "I have decided to follow Jesus, no turning back, no turning back."

Cynthia was quiet on the walk back to the main building, the words flowing through her mind like peaceful running water. It was a thrill to her soul as well as a challenge.

"Why so pensive?" Reg asked.

"Oh, I'm sorry. But that last song really got to me . . . it was a challenge . . . I do so want to live a life pleasing to God."

Reg took her hand in his, pulled her off the paved path, turned her to face him and said, "You are a very special person, Cynthia. I believe if that is the desire of your heart, He will help you."

"I believe it too, Reg," she assured him.

"Cynthia, I have to be out of town for most of next week. There is a political meeting in Iowa I want to attend; besides, I have a personal matter to think over and pray about and I need to be away to do that objectively. I'll call you as soon as I return."

Spontaneously she blurted out, "I'll miss you, Reg."

"Will you, Cynthia? I hope you do." Stooping, he kissed her lightly, gently on the forehead. "I'll miss you, too."

His kiss was so unexpected that Cynthia was not prepared for her reaction to it. Her heart beat faster, then settled down again as she told herself it was like the kiss of an affectionate brother. Next she thought with a quick swell of bitterness, she really didn't know what an affectionate brother's kiss could be like! The bitterness was quickly quelled as they started along the path hand in hand, with her heart once again beating to the refrain of, "I have decided to follow Jesus,"—that meant forgiveness.

As they approached the apartment, Cynthia spoke, "Pray for me, Reg, that I'll find God's will for my life and be willing to follow Him, whatever the cost to me."

"Don't worry, you'll be constantly in my thoughts and prayers. I'll call you as soon as I return."

"I'll be waiting for your call," she said.

Sunday afternoon, following the midday meal with Matt and Kate, Cynthia went to her room, anxious to start reading the book of Colossians. Heaping pillows behind her on the bed, she eagerly opened her Bible and began reading. Taking the time to read every marked footnote, her yearning heart, which had been filled to the point of bursting with bitterness and the need to be accepted, was exulting with the comforting words she read so avidly about the grace of God. 'Nobody deserves to have the love of God. Nevertheless, God loves the sinner and has provided the way of salvation. This is the manifestation of God's grace. It is His free gift.' A feeling of awe filled her soul as she thought—and this includes me!!

As she continued reading, she was delighted to read once again that God had created all things . . . and for His glory. As she read on, totally engrossed, she came to the verse in the second chapter that startled her. 'Beware lest any man spoil you through philosophy and vain deceit, after the tradition of man, after the rudiments of the world and not after Christ.' The footnotes described 'rudiments' as religious rites and 'world' as mankind.

Marveling that all of this was in God's Word, she told herself, "This describes Ted Black and his followers exactly." Pausing a moment, she lifted a thankful heart to God in gratitude for rescuing her from that misguided group.

Eagerly, she read on. There was so much to grasp, but a few more verses stood out for her.

. . . 'If ye then be risen with Christ seek those things which are above . . .' She exclaimed aloud as she read verses 12 and 13 of chapter 3, 'Put on therefore as the elect of God, holy and beloved, bowels of mercy, kindness, humbleness of mind, meekness, longsuffering: Forbearing one another and forgiving one another, if any man have a quarrel against any: even as Christ forgave you so also do ye.'

Trembling, she thought, here it is again. Looking up 'bowels of mercy,' she found it meant from the heart or innermost being, and here was the forgiving part again. She paused once more to beseech her Heavenly Father to take complete possession of her heart to help her to love her mother; not just forgive her but to actually love her. Was it possible? As Gramps had told her, God does not ask the impossible of us . . . then she thought once again of the admonition, 'lean not to thine own understanding . . .'

She read on, 'And whatsoever ye do in word or deed, do all in the name of the Lord Jesus.'

She sat for a long time communing with her Heavenly Father . . . while the things of earth she had thought so important faded away . . . and the desire to please God growing stronger until a deepening peace filled her being.

It seemed that her day was really spiritually fulfilled as she attended the final meeting with the Miller family . . . at the closing they sang 'Wonderful Peace,' a song from the hymnal, asking everyone to join in the chorus.

As she sang with the rest, the words were so meaningful they brought tears to her eyes. 'Peace, peace, wonderful peace; coming down from the Father above. Sweep over my spirit forever I pray, In fathomless billows of love.'

No longer rejected! Oh, what a loving Lord she had found!

CHAPTER SEVENTEEN

Cynthia didn't have time to miss Reg the following week as the teens from the inner city kept them all busy. Finally realizing that they all liked pasta, they tried to arrange that kind of meals. With the added help they brought along, it was easy. One jolly Italian man made wonderful pasta dishes, always urging Cynthia to sample them as she consulted with him about the daily orders.

"Might as well give these kids what they like. Won't waste food that way. Pasta's good for them, anyway. I mix in meat and other nutritious foods and they don't know the difference. And if they all like ice cream ... so what ... saves baking," he commented with a deep belly laugh.

Jason was needed with the group to help discipline the morning meetings, so Cynthia stayed in the office in his place. It was a busy but rewarding week, as she no longer felt alienated from her co-workers.

Friday night Reg called. "Hi, I'm back. How

about going on a picnic with me tomorrow? It is your day off, isn't it?"

"Yes, it is and I'd love to go with you, Reg."

"How would you like to take a boat ride on Lake Champlain?"

Her eyes sparkled. "I'd love it—I guess—I haven't been on the water much."

"A friend of mine has a small cruiser. I'll see if I can borrow it. I'll call for you around one o'clock, okay?"

"That's fine, I'll be ready," she assured him happily.

Now, what to wear in a boat! Guess I'd better wear slacks. She rummaged through her closet Saturday morning and found a white pair. Choosing a three-quarter-length tunic in wide blue and white stripes, she then found a pair of blue sneakers. Satisfied with her selections, she ate breakfast, found Kate and told her where she was going, and was ready for Reg when he arrived.

"Hey, we look like twins," he laughed. He, too, was wearing white duck pants, a blue and white pullover, white sneakers and a white sailor cap set jauntily on his wavy brown hair.

"So we do," she smiled. Remembering her first impression of him, she wondered how she could ever have thought he was just an average person—in any way.

It turned out to be a beautiful summer day. Sometimes the lake could be rough, but today its blue waters only rippled in the wake of a gentle breeze.

The boat was a lovely thing, white with black leather seats and trimmings. A wide windshield protected them from the spray from other crafts. A convertible-style top of canvas could be easily put into place enclosing them, Reg explained, in the event it rained or the sun was too hot.

First of all, after they were away from the wharf, he had to show her the speed of which the boat was capable. She loved it even though the wind blew her hair into tangles. But most of all, she liked the times when they just cruised and could converse above the roar of the motor without shouting.

"Half of the lake—or at least a part of it—belongs to New York State." He then went on to tell her briefly about the history of the lake. French explorer, Samuel de Champlain, discovered the lake in 1609. For 150 years the French, Dutch and English battled to control the 110-mile waterway, the sixth largest fresh water lake in the United States. An American fleet finally ended the conflict, winning a naval battle during the war of 1812.

Canals had linked the lake to the Hudson and St. Lawrence rivers when steamer and barge traffic had kept the waters busy with commerce. The steamer, Vermont, was launched in 1805, the first of a fleet of 29 paddlewheelers that cruised the lake for over a century.

"You can see how it has changed today by the power boats, the ferries, the sightseeing cruisers, the fishing boats, and other recreational activities."

"It certainly is beautiful," Cynthia enthused.

"It can really be rough on a windy day, though. We chose a perfect day. Hey, do you realize it's 5:30? I'm starved, how about you? Let's eat, shall we?"

"Sounds wonderful. I'm ravenous. This open air, I suppose. But where will we eat?"

"I'll just drop anchor and we'll eat right here. It seems to be quiet enough, and I can pull close to shore where we'll be under the shade of the overhanging branches."

"My, you've thought of everything, even this wide-brimmed hat for me for which I am very grateful," she remarked as he reached for an insulated food basket and two thermos bottles.

Opening the basket, Reg pulled out a small cloth which he spread on the seat between them. Then, carefully he removed packaged rolls, plastic dishes of cubed cucumbers, barbecued potato chips, carrot and celery sticks, and large Spanish olives.

"That all looks scrumptious," Cynthia said hungrily.

Reaching across the back of the seat, he clasped one of her hands in his while he thanked the Lord for His goodness and provision for them.

Handing her a wrapped roll he said anxiously, "Hope you like crabmeat."

"I love it," she enthused, unwrapping it and taking a big bite. "Ummm," she sighed as she relaxed. "Hits the spot." It sounded so funny coming from her overly-filled mouth, they almost choked on their spontaneous laughter.

"I thought seafood was called for on this nautical excursion," he joshed.

"Indeed, sir, indeed," she agreed, reaching for a chip.

They ate in silence for a time, lazily watching sailboats and other cruisers in the distance.

"What mountain range is that?" Cynthia asked, indicating the high uneven crest of timber across the lake.

"The Adirondacks. It's a busy place for campers and hikers."

"Looks enchanting," she answered lazily, "but I can't believe it could be nicer than The Farm. Oh, these rolls are so-o-o good. I think I'll have another one," she said, reaching for one.

Reg brought out huge cold peaches for dessert. They had a merry time eating them, they were so juicy. It took loads of napkins to keep the juice from dripping off their chin, which sent them into gales of laughter for no really good reason.

When they docked at Reg's friend's mooring place, the sun was just dipping behind the mountain, casting a deep bronze glow over everything, causing even the boat and shoreline to reflect its color.

Reg gave his companion an admiring glance as he helped her from the boat. "The reflection from the sun makes your hair look like gold, Cindy. It's beautiful."

"Why, thank you, Reg," she smiled demurely. "We are going to miss the meeting at the chapel tonight."

"I know, and I'm sorry, but it has been such an enjoyable day that time just got away from me."

She responded lightheartedly, "You are forgiven for this time."

Later in her room, reflecting on the events of the afternoon, she realized the only intimate moment—if one could really call it that—was when Reg had made the remark about her hair.

Stopping short while brushing the tangles from her tresses, she thought, why, I'm falling in love with him! Panic hit her. But I must not do that—tossing her brush aside she crawled into bed. "Lord, help me not to be so foolish—help me to keep my heart from wanting something or someone you don't want me to have"—but she fell asleep with a smile on her face—Reg is such a nice—no, not just nice—such a super person . . .

Monday at four when Cynthia reported for work at the office, a letter had arrived from her dad. As soon as she had time, she opened it.

"Dear Cindy, your letter quite surprised us, but I am very happy for you. I keep thinking how fortunate you were to go to Matt and Kate.

"I have a two-week vacation the second and third weeks in September. Would you make a reservation for me at The Farm? I would like to see you and really get to know your uncle. Let me know as soon as you can if you have room for me. Your mother can't come. She is enclosing a note. I'm not sure what it will say, but bear with her, Cindy. She has been very quiet since we got your letter.

"Oliver is thinking of joining the navy and this makes her quite upset.

"Ted Black was here one day recently, asking for your address and I'm glad I was home, although I don't think your mother would have given it to him, either. I told him you were away and I was positive you wouldn't care to hear from him. He seemed to be so sure you would be interested in what he called an 'exciting new concept in religion.' Did I do the right thing? Love, Dad."

She certainly did not want to hear from Ted Black ever again! She was thankful her dad understood her.

Uncle Matt and Aunt Kate would be delighted that her dad was coming here, and she herself thought that now she could get to know him. She knew there would be a vacancy by the registry, and Lydia had told her that these two weeks were always slow—between Labor Day and the foliage season.

She had been holding her mother's note, dreading to read it, but finally decided not to put it off any longer. Unfolding it, she read, "Dear Cynthia, your letter didn't really surprise me. I hope you will not be disappointed in this religion. Your father says he's coming there next month. It is impossible for me to join him. We are having bake sales to pay the expenses of our bridge club members' annual trip to Florida, as we always do.

"As for our relationship, I must admit it never has been the way I wanted it to be. It always seemed to me from the time Oliver was born that you have been cool toward me, never heeding my advice, always resentful about obeying, and I always wondered why. But now you have moved away, and I suggest we forget the whole matter and go on from here. Yours truly, Your Mother."

Tears formed in Cynthia's eyes as she read between the lines. Yes, she had been at fault somewhat, but evidently her mother had never realized how much she had put Oliver first. No matter, now she would try, with God's help, to go on from here and do her best to forget the past and to even learn to love her mother. Meanwhile, she was thrilled that her dad was coming to see her.

She looked through the reservations for rooms available and reserved a single room for him.

Having time, she answered the letter, sticking strictly to details. "Happy you are coming, Dad. I've reserved a room for you. Wish you could come too, Mother. Dad, I never want to see or hear from Ted Black again. You did exactly the right thing. Love, Cindy." She then placed the letter with the mail just as Don came on duty.

Her morning duties seemed to take longer that day; therefore, it was not until noon that she found time to tell her relatives that her dad was coming to The Farm for two weeks.

"That's wonderful," Matt seemed excited. "I'll be so happy to get to know Norman better. We will have to start the prayer group praying for his salvation while he's here. I think I can manage a day or two off, also, although there are usually odds and ends of things to do during our slack times, which are becoming fewer and fewer."

"I've put him in a room close by you two," she informed them. Then she told of her mother's note, stating, "I believe she and I can have a better relationship, but somehow I feel as if it will never be close—unless she comes to know Christ."

"And that's not impossible, Cindy," Kate said firmly.

"No—not impossible," Cynthia agreed.

"We haven't had a chance to talk since your outing Saturday. Did you enjoy the day?"

"It was fantastic," Cynthia replied with exuberance. "Reg is such fun to be with."

Tuesday evening Reg came to the chapel meeting. It was a beautiful evening, the half-circle silvery moon enhancing the canopy of a dark blue velvet sky. The air was quite balmy for this late August date.

As they were leaving the chapel, Reg asked

Cynthia, "How about going somewhere for a pizza or something? It's such a beautiful night, too nice to go in."

"Well—" she hesitated, "if we're not too late."

"I know a good place for a snack only a few miles from here. We won't be late, I promise."

Seated at a table later, eating apple pie ala mode, Cynthia told Reg about her dad coming.

"That's nice. I'd like to meet him," before adding, "Cindy, Alex and Ellyn have invited the singles group to their home for dinner this Thursday at seven o'clock. Will you go with me?"

"I'd love to go, but you don't need to take me, it's only a short distance from here."

"But I want you to go with me. I'd like to call for you."

"Okay, sounds like fun. I've wanted to see their home. I've heard it's gorgeous, and I like both of them—what little I know of them."

Leaving her later, he merely said, "See you a little before seven on Thursday."

The following evening, Cynthia asked Joan Fisher if she planned to go to the Harrisons' on Thursday.

Joan grinned impishly. "Wouldn't miss it," she quipped.

"What do we wear? Will it be formal?"

"I'd say semi— just a dressy dress, if you know what I mean."

So that afternoon Cynthia went shopping for a new dress. After an hour of searching, she found just what she wanted in a small dress shoppe in Burlington. A shirtwaist-style of shimmering silk Jersey in her favorite mint green. The buttons were iridescent, flashing different colors, enhancing its plainness. The skirt was mid-calf length and full, with a wide belt.

Reg stared when he saw her. Finally he spoke. "You look stunning, Cindy."

"Thank you kindly, sir," she smiled as she slid

her hand through his proffered arm as he walked her to the car. Helping her in he closed the door, and moving quickly slid into the driver's seat.

The Harrisons had truly prepared for their guests. Chilled juices and a variety of hors d'oeuvres were served in the living room. At 7:30 dinner was announced by the maid. Alex offered prayer before the four-course meal was served.

At the close of the meal, Alex stood to speak. "Ellyn and I have a two-fold purpose for entertaining this group tonight. The first is because we enjoy having young people around us, and the second is to announce the engagement of my son in the faith, Kenneth Ross, to Miss Joan Fisher."

While he had been speaking, the maid was placing goblets of sparkling grape juice at each place.

"Let's toast the happy couple. Ken—Joan, we congratulate both of you and wish you a long and happy marriage as you serve the Lord together."

After the toast the group looked pointedly at Ken and chanted, "Speech—speech!"

A beaming Ken stood to his feet, pulling Joan up beside him. "I want to thank Alex and Ellyn for this lovely evening. I feel that, indeed, I am to be congratulated because this lovely young lady has promised to share my life. But it won't be for a year. Joan has another year of college, and I need to be sure where the Lord wants me to serve Him."

A noise-filled happy time followed as the couple was congratulated by their friends, with lots of sly remarks like, "I suppose you thought we would be surprised," and "You two thought we didn't know—ha, ha." The newly-engaged couple only grinned and replied in kind.

As the party broke up, they all thanked their hosts for a delightful evening. When Reg drove into the parking lot at The Farm, he said, "Could we talk a few minutes, Cynthia?"

"Why, of course. What about?"

"Are you sure that Ted Black means nothing

to you?" he asked bluntly.

"Ted Black? Who's he?"

"Seriously, Cindy."

"Seriously, Reg. He is out of my life for good. I think the only reason, as I told you before, I even got involved with that group in the first place was because they made me feel—wanted. But, Reg, now that I know God, I no longer feel unwanted or rejected."

After a moment he spoke again. "I suppose you know that I have a reputation of being a 'love 'em and leave 'em' type."

"Yup, I have heard that."

"It's not true, basically. I've never led a girl on, allowing her to think I was serious. There was one girl who taught in our Christian school for a year, but after a very short time we both knew we wouldn't be more than friends. When she left to go on to another job, we parted as good friends. I was teased a lot, but both she and I, and God, knew the truth."

"I think your very best friends like the Holloways, the Jeff Roberts and the Phillips all know the truth, Reg."

"Cynthia, I've never before asked a girl to marry me. I love you, Cindy. Do you think you could love me—in time? I almost asked you the day we went on the boat ride, but I thought it was too soon. Maybe it still is—too soon—is it, Cindy?"

"I've been trying to say yes, if you would stop chattering, Reg," she said with a smile. "Yes, I'll marry you."

"I thought it was too soon—what!" he shouted. "Did you say yes?"

She laughed a happy, joyous laugh. "I said yes. I love you, too."

He stared at her for a moment, the nearby lawn light illuminating his astonishment as it turned to delight.

Drawing her gently into his arms, he cradled

her head on his shoulder for a moment before he tilted her face for his kiss. "Oh, my darling, I was so afraid you'd refuse me. Oh, Cindy, I love you so dearly."

"And I you, my darling," she responded.

Fumbling in his pocket, he drew out a small box. "Then you'll wear this? I want everyone to know you are promised to me."

As he slid the diamond ring onto her engagement finger, she said, "It's beautiful, darling. I'll be proud to wear it."

"How soon can we be married? Right away? My folks will be so pleased. When?" he urged.

"But we've only just become engaged, Reg."

"No matter. I want my wife to accompany me to Montpelier this winter. I can't wait to show you off."

"Oh, I forgot about you being a senator. I'm not accustomed to being in society like that. Will I fit in?"

"You'd fit in anywhere, honey."

"If you say so," she responded happily, before laying her head contentedly on his shoulder once again.

By the time she went inside, they had set a tentative date for the wedding the Saturday after Thanksgiving.

"That will give us time for a decent honeymoon before the legislature convenes."

But Cynthia was so ecstatic she couldn't think beyond this very evening—this time of new awakening love—so precious, as Reg had said—made especially so between two believers.

CHAPTER EIGHTEEN

The phone rang the following morning just as Jason entered the office. Upon answering it, he said, "It's for you, Miss Marsh."

With raised eyebrows she took the receiver and said, "Yes, this is Miss Marsh."

"Why so formal, darling?" came Reg's voice.

"How could I know it would be you?" she answered, looking guardedly at Jason.

His voice came again. "Mother wants you to come to dinner tonight. How about it? They are very pleased about us, sweetheart."

"If you're sure, I'd love it," she laughed shakily. Everything seemed to be happening so fast . . .

"It'll just be the four of us. I'll come by for you promptly at six and, darling, I can hardly wait."

"Same here," she answered feeling an inward warmth.

Replacing the receiver, she said hastily, "See you at four, Jason." She wanted to tell her relatives the good news first before anyone else.

Running up the front stairs, she hurried to the linen room. Good, she thought, Kate was there. "Aunt Kate, I have something to tell you. Reg asked me to marry him last night and I said yes. See my ring?"

Kate stood with her mouth gaping. "Well, I never! I knew you were good friends, but this!—it's great news, Cindy. I'm so pleased. Reg is such a fine young man. Does Uncle Matt know?"

"Not yet. I'm on my way to find him now. I wanted you two to be the first to know. I'm so happy, Aunt Kate. We are being married the Saturday after Thanksgiving. See you later. I'm going to be late for work."

Rushing out to the shop, she related her news to her uncle. He was as delighted as Kate had been.

As she met Ken Ross for their daily conference, he noticed her ring right away. "Hey, what gives, Cindy?"

Blushing from a sense of shyness, she answered, "Reg and I are to be married, Ken. At Thanksgiving time."

"Hey, that's no fair. Even before Joan and me! No kidding, though, Cindy, Reg is really a dedicated Christian and a great guy. He's been so friendly to me this summer. And now that you are a Christian, too, I think it's great! Wait till I tell Joan. Will she ever be surprised. God bless you both."

When she told Lydia and Gramps, they were as surprised and pleased as everyone else had been.

Dressing carefully for the dinner date, she suddenly felt nervous. Then she prayed, "Lord, let them like me if it's Your will. I've never been so happy in my life as now. With You as my guide and Reg as my husband—who could ask for more? Thank You, Lord."

As they drove to the Thomas home Reg, noticing that Cynthia was clasping and unclasping her hands, asked, "Nervous, dear?"

"Yes," she admitted, "a little. What if they

don't like me?"

"They will, don't worry. You see, all they want is my happiness and now they know that it is with you as my wife, they will love you, too. Cindy, I never knew that being in love could be so wonderful. You are the girl I've been waiting for—oh, perhaps not consciously, but I knew right away you were the one—but I had to wait until you came to the Saviour, because as the Word says, 'How can two walk together unless they be agreed?' So, don't be nervous, sweetheart, relax."

"Okay, I'll try, but I'll be glad when we get there."

Reg was right. His mother greeted Cynthia with outstretched hands. "My dear, we are so thrilled that Reggie has finally decided to get married, and to such a lovely girl."

"Thank you," Cynthia replied shyly. "I love him dearly, you know."

"We couldn't ask for more, could we?" Lucy Thomas beamed. Leaning over, she kissed Cynthia lightly on her cheek. Then taking each of them by the hand she said, "Let's join Dad in the den."

Ralph Thomas greeted Cynthia with as much enthusiasm as his wife had. "It's about time this son of ours settled down."

"I had to find the right girl first, Dad," Reg protested.

"Oh, I know that, son. Anyway, we are delighted." Turning to his wife he said, "Is dinner ready, Lucy? I'm famished."

"All ready, Ralph. I just have to put it on the table. Give me five minutes."

"Can I help?" Cynthia offered.

"Not this time, dear, but thanks anyway. I'll no doubt accept your help many times in the future. It's only a simple family meal tonight."

When they were called to dinner, Mrs. Thomas explained, "I thought we'd eat in the small dining room tonight. This is where we eat when we're alone, and as you are going to be one of the family, Cynthia, I thought it would be more cozy."

"I appreciate your thoughtfulness, Mrs. Thomas."

Her hostess smiled. "We'll have to work on that Mrs. Thomas bit—it sounds too formal for the relationship I hope we'll develop between us, Cindy."

After the father of the home asked the blessing, they all ate hungrily of the delicious meal which consisted of chilled apple juice, crisp loin pork roast with light-as-a-feather stuffing, fluffy baked potatoes, hot spicy applesauce, fresh peas smothered in butter, fresh baby carrots and pineapple chunks in a creamy sauce and tiny dinner rolls, topped off with raspberry sherbet.

While they ate, they chatted amiably. Cynthia discovered that Reg had told them about her dad coming for a visit.

"You must bring your father to dinner while he is here, Cindy. We are looking forward to meeting him."

Feeling suddenly stifled, breathless, thinking, how will Dad fit into this environment, she blurted out, "Dad is only a foreman in a machine shop, you know."

Ralph Thomas spoke quickly. "And what is that supposed to mean?"

Cynthia flushed and stammered, "We are just common people—I just—just wondered—you understand I've never been close to my family—if he would—fit in."

Ralph spoke again, gently this time. "Cynthia, when one is a Christian there is no distinction of class, if I understand you correctly. God is no respecter of persons so how can we be? Each one of us is born into our own distinctive place—it just so happened that my grandfather built this house and I inherited it from my father as Reg will from me, Lord willing. I also inherited the business—otherwise I might never have been even a foreman of anything. Never be ashamed of your family, Cynthia.

As I said before, we look forward to meeting your father."

Her face turned red then white as she listened. "Oh, I'm not ashamed of my father. It's not that." She looked appealingly at Reg.

"It's okay, dear, let's talk about something else. If we're finished eating, I'd like to show Cindy the house."

"A good idea, son," his mother said.

Cynthia was subdued and very quiet as Reg led her from one room to another. The spacious dining room with its elegant furnishings and rich Oriental rug impressed her. "How many people can you entertain here at one time?" she asked.

"We have had up to twenty."

The huge living room was elegantly yet tastefully furnished and boasted a massive fireplace and huge bay window. She had seen the den "which is really where we live," Reg explained. They peeked into the master bedroom which Reg told her had its own bath and walk-in closet. There were two other bedrooms on the first floor with connecting baths.

Leading her into a hallway, they ascended to the second floor. Reg flung open a door explaining, "My room, also with my own bath."

Another bedroom was disclosed before they crossed the hallway. "We don't use this apartment now, but my grandparents lived here after Dad married. It's been closed for some time. There are two bedrooms, a bath, living room, dining room, and a huge kitchen which needs remodeling badly." Brushing dust off the wide bay window seat directly over the one on the lower floor, Reg pulled her down beside him. "Cindy, my parents would like us to take over the first floor and they move up here after we're married. It's been a tradition in the family since my great-grandparents lived up here. What do you think, dear? I don't want you to feel pressured."

She stammered, "I'm so confused with all of this luxury, I can't think right now—but, Reg, why couldn't we live up here—your parents aren't old enough to leave their home yet—let me think about it. My first thought is that I'd like it better up here— for now, anyway."

"You're sure you wouldn't like a home by ourselves? I can manage that, if you'd rather," he asked anxiously.

"Do we have to decide tonight?"

"Of course not. I'll tell the folks I've presented the plan to you and we will be praying about it. In fact, why don't we ask the Lord's guidance right now."

After he prayed, they went downstairs where the elder Thomases were eagerly awaiting them. Cynthia noticed the questioning look his mother gave Reg and his slight negative response. She was relieved, she needed time to think about all this . . .

The young couple soon wandered outside through the patio. Cynthia sank onto a settee and Reg dropped quickly down beside her. She looked so perplexed that he reassured her, "Take your time, honey, there's no hurry."

"Thank you, dear. Now let's enjoy this lovely sunset. Is it always as gorgeous as this?"

"Not always. I'm glad it is tonight. It is the perfect ending for a perfect day, to quote an old cliche."

Leaning her head on his shoulder, where she was quickly learning it fitted perfectly, she remarked, "Everything seems tinted with the beautiful sunset tonight, or is it the glow of contentment I feel enhancing everything?"

"Perhaps it is both," he murmured, drawing her into a tender embrace.

Later, on their way to The Farm, Reg said, "I'd like you to attend church with me Sunday, Cindy. I am quite active there and that's where our home church will be."

"I'd like that and, Reg, Gramps said something to me about being baptized, also."

"We have to talk with the pastor about the wedding plans anyway, so we'll ask him about that at the same time."

"Were any other two people ever as happy as we are, Reg?"

"I suppose so, but it does seem as though we have an edge on it, my darling."

The following two weeks before Labor Day were hectic and exciting. The Holloways and Harrisons were busy with visiting relatives. Jason wanted Cynthia to meet his grandparents and Jerry wanted her to meet his family, so Andrea threw another party inviting the Paige family also, who were at The Farm for their usual vacation.

Cynthia was impressed with Pamela Paige's singing, as she was the soloist at many of the meetings.

"What a terrific voice she has, Reg. So deep and mellow. She'll no doubt have a great future ahead of her. But one thing has amused me and that is the way she hangs around Jason. I teased him about it this morning and he just laughed and said he couldn't help it if his boyish charm slayed all the girls. But I'm sure it's not amusing to Pamela the way she hangs on his every word."

"Maybe you're only imagining things," was Reg's response.

"Maybe," she laughed, "but I'm not imagining the romance between Jerry and Gretchen. After the party at Andrea's, Gretchen told me that both sets of parents had agreed to let them have an understanding to get engaged as soon as they graduate from high school. Then they plan to attend the same music school and after that, get married and serve the Lord together with their musical talents. They seem awfully young to have their lives already planned."

"Look at Jeff and Sylvia, they were high school sweethearts and their marriage is certainly a success," Reg pointed out.

"That's true," she agreed.

Cynthia was meeting each week with the deacons of the church for baptismal classes, and she and Reg were to start premarital counseling with the pastor the middle of September.

Labor Day saw the usual exodus from The Farm with changes in personnel as well. Mark Randall, a university student, returned to take over for Don Nobles at the front desk. Mark didn't leave until 7:00 a.m. so Cynthia no longer needed to get up at dawn. A lady from the local church agreed to come in from 8:30 to 2:00 each day while her children were in school, so Cynthia would take over from 2:00 to 4:00 until Mark returned from the university. Mark would work weekends, also.

One day Cynthia asked her boss, "Do you think I'm leaving you in the lurch, Lydia? Even though you've assured me it's okay, I still feel as though, after all you've done for me, I am letting you down."

"Don't give it another thought. The snack bar will be closed and dorm activities will be much less, and the Lord always supplies our needs. We'll miss you, Cindy, but we're so happy for you. I understand you are to live in an apartment in the Thomas home."

"Yes, we are. Reg and I have been looking at remodeling plans for the kitchen and bathroom and Cory Phillips has promised to put a crew in there soon. He said it will be completed before we return from our wedding trip. I'm so happy, Lydia. Just think, if I hadn't come here I probably would never have found God nor met Reg."

"But you did. Our God works in wondrous ways," Lydia replied.

But all was not rosy. On the day Norman Marsh was due to arrive, Cynthia received a disturbing phone call. She was busy on second floor helping to sort bed linen when she was paged.

"Cynthia—Cynthia Marsh, you have a phone call, please answer on the extension up there."

Rushing to the phone she wondered who could be calling her at that time of day—had something happened to her dad? Breathlessly she gasped, "Hello, Cynthia speaking."

"Cynthia, I've had a dreadful time locating you but at last I've found you."

Astounded, she almost dropped the receiver. "Ted—Ted Black!"

"Who else?" he laughed. "I've missed you, Cindy."

"I find that hard to believe—how is Ethel?"

"Oh, that's all off. I took her to her folks' home and then went on my vacation. I thought I'd give you time to miss me, then I'd take you back—but your folks refused to give me your address."

"Then how did you find me?" she asked icily.

"Oliver told me where you were and I called Information and finally located you. I have the most fantastic news for you. It's all so exciting . . ."

"Just a minute, Ted, I am the one who has fantastic news . . ."

"But it can't possibly be as exciting as mine," he interrupted. "Cindy, I forgive you for all of your shortcomings. You see, I've since discovered that only one in each group should be the higher god and, of course, that's me. Ethel disagreed and left to start her own group because she wanted to be equal to me, and I couldn't have that."

"Just like Lucifer," Cynthia murmured.

"What was that? What did you say?"

"I said just like Lucifer who wanted to be equal with the one true God. I discovered God, Ted, and He did make us in His image—but for us to worship **Him**—not ourselves . . ."

"What utter nonsense!" he shouted.

"Of course it would be to you, but not to me. I'm a Christian, Ted. I've accepted God's Son, the Lord Jesus, as my Saviour."

"Are you crazy?" he shouted again.

"I've never been more sane or as happy in my life as I am right now."

"But, Cindy, I've just returned from a conference on the West Coast and I've learned that if we strive hard enough and do the right things that we need not fear death because we can come back to earth and be whatever we want to be. And . . ."

"Ted, listen to me. My future is all secure in Jesus. I know my destiny is in Heaven with Him and when He returns I will be with Him because I belong to Him."

"How utterly ridiculous," he was shouting again. "Cindy, come back home and . . ."

"This is a pointless conversation, Ted. I feel sorry for you."

"Sorry! For me! Don't be silly."

"Yes, sorry. You are like the blind leading the blind. You are an emissary for the Devil, and unless you find the one true God, your destiny is Hell—everlasting punishment."

"Why—why how dare you . . ."

"Because it's true. I'm hanging up, Ted. Don't contact me again—ever—unless you want to know the one true God, and if that happens I'll put you in touch with someone who can help you." With that she hung up.

Kate, who had entered the linen room just a moment before, asked, "What was that all about?"

Cynthia burst into laughter which quickly turned to tears. "That was Ted. He—he wants me back—oh, Aunt Kate, it scares me to think I ever even liked him or believed him."

"There, there, dear, it's okay now."

When she had quieted down she said, "How thankful I am that God delivered me from that evil cult and brought me to Himself. It gives me the shivers whenever I think of the narrow escape I had—and to think that arrogant man would think all he had to do was whistle and I'd come running back! Humph! Fat chance!"

"But he's a soul for whom Christ died," Kate reminded her gently.

"Oh, I know, but it'll be some miracle if Ted ever recognizes any God but himself."

"Forget it for now, Cindy. Let's finish this linen count so we will know how much to order, and then it will be lunch time."

As they worked, Kate asked, "What time are you meeting Norman?"

"Five, at the bus stop in town. You know, Aunt Kate, it's really getting to me that I have no home to entertain Reg in. We have to either go out to eat, or to his home, or bowling or something. We are taking Dad out for dinner tonight, somewhere."

"It won't be for long. I wish we had a larger place."

With a rueful grin, Cynthia said, "Forgive me for grumbling, Aunt Kate. I'm truly grateful for all you and Uncle Matt have done for me."

Later at the bus depot, Cynthia and Reg waited. The bus was late. It was 5:30 before it finally arrived. The bus was crowded and Mr. Marsh was one of the last to appear. Cynthia rushed to meet him with Reg directly behind her.

"It's so good to see you, Dad. This all of your luggage?" she asked, indicating his one large bag.

"Yes, that's it. How are you, Cindy?" he asked, kissing her on the cheek.

"Just fine. Dad, I'd like you to meet a friend of mine, Reginald Thomas. Reg, my father, Norman Marsh."

Reginald grasped the older man's hand firmly. "How was your trip, sir?"

"Nice, except very tiring."

"We thought we'd grab a bite to eat first before we bring you to The Farm. Okay, Dad?"

He smiled. "Of course, Cindy."

"How does a steak sound, Mr. Marsh?" Reg inquired, smiling.

"Great. I'm sure that's just what I need to

revive me. That and a hot cup of coffee."

"Let's go, then," Reg said, grabbing the suitcase.

As they drove to the steak house, Cynthia was regretting very much the decision she had made not to tell her father of her engagement to Reg until after they had met. Reg had been upset by it, as she had removed her ring that night until she told her father.

Once their order was placed and they were seated at a table sipping hot coffee, Cynthia talked incessantly—almost nervously—until Reg went to collect their steaks and her dad asked if anything was troubling her. "Is Mr. Thomas a special friend, Cindy?"

"Yes, he is, Dad," relieved that Reg was back with their meal.

The steaks were delicious, as usual, and they ate leisurely. Cynthia had quieted down, allowing the men to become acquainted. After a slow, stilted start, they soon were conversing amiably, for which she was grateful.

Arriving at The Farm, Reg drew Cynthia aside as Matt and Kate welcomed Norman, and whispered sternly, "Tell him before tomorrow night or I'll think you don't really love me."

"I will, I promise." He started to kiss her but she pushed him away. "Sorry, darling, I really am, and now I wish I'd told him before, but . . ." she shrugged and said, "Good night," feeling upset because she knew she had hurt him.

As it happened, she told her dad that very night. After a brief chat with Matt and Kate, Cynthia took her father to the reservation desk. Mark had his card all ready so it was only formality. She then returned with him upstairs. Once inside his room, she closed the drapes, turned down his bed and started to say good night. Instead, she blurted out, "Dad, I have something to tell you which I am very sorry I haven't told you and Mother before—but I wanted you to meet Reg and get to know him first. Dad, he has asked me to marry him and I have accepted. I love him very much."

A hurt look crept into her dad's eyes as she spoke. "How long has it been?"

"Only a short time—about two weeks. Please Dad, try to understand."

"I'm trying to, Cindy, but it hurts to think you would keep something so important from us."

"Dad," she pleaded, "I am truly sorry. Reg is cross with me about it, too. Please forgive me and be happy for me."

Drawing her into his arms he said gently, "Of course I forgive you, child. When I call your mother tomorrow may I tell her?"

"Of course," she readily agreed, "unless," she added uneasily, "you think I should call her."

"No-o-o, I think I can make her understand. We'll see."

"We plan to be married on November 25th in Reg's home church here."

"So soon? Well, you always have made your own decisions, at least for some years now. What about Ted?"

"Dad, he had the audacity to call me—just today! Oliver told him where I was. He treated me badly, Dad, but I thank God I'm out from under his terrible influence. Reginald is a wonderful Christian. He is a state senator, and sells insurance and real estate with his father."

"I do like him—so far. I'm dead tired now, Cindy. We'll talk more tomorrow. I'm glad you told me tonight."

"Okay, see you in the morning."

"Kate asked me to eat breakfast with them but I told her I thought I'd like to sleep in. The bus trip was very tiring."

"Then how about me meeting you around 8:30 in the dining room and we'll eat together?"

"Sounds good, Cindy. I really think I'm going

to like it here."

"I know you will, Dad, and I'm so glad you came."

CHAPTER NINETEEN

The days reeled by so rapidly, Cynthia felt as though she were being carried along by a whirlwind. As her dad became acquainted with Reg, she could see that he came to like him. Not only that, but Ralph and Lucy Thomas welcomed him into their home with such warmth that Cynthia's already happy heart was filled to overflowing with the sweetness of Christian fellowship.

Reg took Norman fishing one day and when they returned, Cynthia knew instantly that they had become good friends. Her whole being flooded with joy the day her dad told her that he had accepted Christ as his Saviour after many talks with Gramps. The one blemish was her mother's response to the announcement of her engagement.

"It seems to me that it's not been long enough between your other marriage plans to be planning another one, but you always have gone your own way and you'll have to lie in the bed you make," was her stiff, unbending reply when Cynthia called her, at her father's request, to tell her the news.

"But, Mother, this is different. Reg is a dedicated Christian and our mutual love for God and each other will be a solid base for a marriage."

"If you say so," came the dry answer, "but you thought the other one was so religious, too."

Sensing her mother could not understand since she wasn't a Christian, Cynthia let that part of the conversation drop and asked, "You will come to my wedding, won't you, Mother?"

"I don't see why you don't come home and get married."

"But we have such a small family and I have so few friends back there and besides, Reg has such a lot of friends from the church and the legislature, we thought it would be best. Mother, please try to understand. Dad is coming to give me away and I do so want you with me on my wedding day."

These words seemed to thaw her mother's heart a bit as she answered, "I'll think about it. Oliver leaves the first of November for training for the Navy. I can't understand that, either."

"I know you'll miss him, Mother, but I do hope you will come with Dad to my wedding."

She had to be satisfied with the promise that was made, to think it over.

When the day came for her father to leave, he was sorry to go. "I only hope I can find a good church to attend. Gramps has given me guidelines to go by."

"I'll be praying for you, Dad. It's been wonderful having you here; for you to get to know Uncle Matt and Aunt Kate, the Roberts family, and most of all Reg and his family."

"I sure can understand why you are so happy here, Cindy. Don't worry about your mother. She'll come around." He smiled wistfully as he tried to joke. "She's actually made me blueberry muffins a few times since you left, and remarked in her offhand way you should be at home to have some.

I believe deep down she loves you, dear."

Tearfully, Cynthia answered, "I do hope so, Dad, but she makes it awfully hard for me. With God's help, I'm trying to feel a genuine love for her. I do long for her salvation."

"We'll have to go slow on that, but we'll all be praying for her. Here comes my bus. Good-bye, dear, until November."

As he shook hands with Reg, he said, "I feel my girl will be happy with you, young man."

Cynthia was rather quiet for a time on the way home. Reg, not speaking either, sensed her need to regain her composure. After a bit he said, "I really like your father, Cindy. He's a real neat guy. We'll pray about your mother—remember nothing, but nothing, is impossible with God."

Casting him a loving glance, she replied, "You are such a comfort to me, sweetheart. And you are right. See what God has done for me in such a short time, and I was next to impossible!"

"Shall we go by the house and see how the remodeling is coming along?"

"Oh, let's," she enthused, snuggling close to him.

The highways were crowded with cars and buses from everywhere, to view the blazing colors of foliage. They were especially brilliant this year, with the different colors blending so perfectly.

"What a prelude to fall," Cynthia declared.

The Farm was filled to capacity, as were all other places in the area accommodating tourists. Cynthia found herself helping out in almost every position. More than once each week the guests overflowed into the new dorm. At times she found herself making up bunk beds. Extra help came in from town and still they were busy—busy.

Even Ken Ross was pressed into service, vacuuming the dorm floor on occasion. One day when she arrived at the dorm he exclaimed, "Guess what, Cindy, I just had a telegram from Alex. He's located my mother."

"How exciting, Ken. A real answer to prayer."

"Yeah. I wonder what she will be like. I hardly remember her. Alex promised to see her and then get in touch again. He's in Los Angeles for a few days."

"We'll pray it will turn out okay, Ken," Cynthia promised.

It turned out to be more than okay. The following day Ken had a telegram from Alex which read, "Talked with your mother. She had given up hope of finding you. Is excited about seeing you. She's coming east with me tomorrow. Meet us at the airport. Don't worry, she's a Christian now. Alex."

"Wow! Things are surely moving fast. I wonder—"

Lydia came hurrying out to the dorm. "Ken, Alex just called me from L.A. He's talked with your mother. She has been searching for you. Meanwhile, she has been working for a daily cleaning service and one of the ladies, a Christian herself, led her to the Lord. Alex knew I was looking for someone to help Kate and asked me if I would consider giving Letha, your mother, a chance. I said yes. Ken, they are arriving tomorrow."

Ken sank into a nearby chair. "Things are really happening fast, aren't they? I'm grateful, Lydia." He laughed shakily. "I'm also nervous."

"Ken, what a wonderful answer to prayer, both for you and Aunt Kate."

"But . . ." Ken muttered.

"No buts—let's just pray it will work out," Lydia stated. "Alex has good judgment. He usually is a good judge of character. You should be able to trust him, too, Ken."

"Of course I do—but it's hit me like a ton of bricks. Where will she stay?"

"Don't worry. I'll find a place for her somewhere." Changing the subject, she asked, "How are you coming here? We have a busload of people due at five o'clock.

Some of the men will be sleeping here."

"We're just about finished, Lydia. I'm due at the office now. I'll have to run and get changed," Cynthia declared.

Ken presented a good message to the guests that evening in spite of his preoccupation concerning meeting his mother the next day—for the first time in years.

Joan had left for college so Ken went by himself to the airport. He thought Ellyn Harrison might go but she had declined.

The scene at the airport was a touching one. Ken and his mother stared at each other, both startled by the appearance of the other. Letha Ross, at 47, was completely white-haired, but had a smooth complexion lending credence to her age, still petite, yet strong-looking. Ken, in turn, was very mature for his 26 years. They barely knew each other. After staring for a couple minutes, Letha threw her arms around her son crying, "Ken—Ken, can you ever forgive me?"

Embracing her in return, he said with misty eyes, "Of course, Mom."

"I'm so proud of you, son. Mr. Harrison, Alex, tells me you are a minister. I'm a Christian, too," she added shyly.

"I know, Mom. We've all been praying for you for a long time now. I think we should join Alex, he'll be anxious to see his family. Lydia, Mrs. Roberts, has insisted you come directly to The Farm. In fact, if you are to help Kate, as I've been informed, they have need of your services right away."

"Let's go, then. Ken, I have much to praise the Lord for, but we'll talk more later."

"As I do, too, Mom. Yes, we'll talk later."

Letha Ross was made welcome at the resort and began working the following morning. Kate liked her. They got along well from the very beginning.

A few nights later at the evening service, which was the only daily service scheduled now (with the exception of Sunday services), Mrs. Ross gave her testimony after Ken told the preliminaries of their separation. Ken kept his eyes on her the whole time. In fact, you could almost have heard a pin drop, such attentiveness prevailed.

At first her voice faltered, but gained strength as she went on. "I have much to praise the Lord for tonight. Ken has told you of the events leading up to the present. I look back and am so sorry I left my family due to my selfishness, especially when Ken really needed a mother, but I was not a good mother at that time." She smiled ruefully. "I thought the world owed me something more than a drunken husband and a delinquent son. Now I can see His hand at work and firmly believe the scripture, 'And we **know** that all things work together for good . . .' We didn't love God then but He was working in all of our lives to help us see our need of Him. I often think that if we had stayed together, had a normal life, we might never have realized our need of a Saviour.

"When I returned to L.A., I found a job with a daily cleaning service—one of the ladies was a Christian who witnessed by her words and her life about the Lord Jesus. I finally saw my need and accepted Him—at last I have found peace of heart. I was searching desperately for my husband and son when Alex Harrison found me. When he told me," with tears streaming down her face and fumbling for a handkerchief she murmured, "excuse me," then went courageously on, —"that Ken was a Christian and that my husband had been saved before he died—you can imagine what a relief it was to me—and then to be offered a job here where I can be near my son and be serving the Lord at the same time. All I can say is—I praise His Name for His love and goodness."

Ken then preached a brief message on the verse, 'Many, O Lord my God, are thy wonderful works which thou hast done, and thy thoughts which are to usward; they cannot be reckoned up in order unto thee: if I would declare and speak of them, they are more than can be numbered.'"

Everyone present sensed the reverence in Ken's words tonight as he elaborated on the wonderful things God had done in his life.

The addition of Letha Ross to the work force left Cynthia free to help elsewhere. Many bus tours wanted boxed lunches to go; she was amazed at the way Lydia was prepared for this. The bakers had used their slack time to fill the freezer with cookies, fruit breads and cupcakes. It was rather exciting in a way, to be involved in this busy time at the resort.

Whenever she had a few free hours, Reg took her driving on his favorite routes to view the beauty of the countryside. She was baptized and joined Reg's church. She and Reg met once a week for premarital counseling.

After one session, Cynthia remarked, "It's a big step, Reg—marriage, isn't it? For a Christian it means a lifetime commitment."

"You'd better believe it, honey," was his answer.

"But, seriously, I mean it, it's a big step, sweetheart. I'm only a new Christian. You'll have to have lots of patience with me."

"Well," he drawled, "I might not be such a new Christian, but contrary to the beliefs of many, I do have a few faults which you might have to have patience with also."

"Seriously, Reg . . ."

"Honey, I know exactly what you mean, but with us both loving the Lord and trying, as the pastor said tonight, to keep the line of communication open between us— It doesn't even seem possible now, but we no doubt will, in time, have minor, I hope, grievances toward each other. We have to keep them in the open and not let them fester. Listen to me! And I am supposed to be a confirmed 'ole bach.' Ha!! Not me. Not now that I've met you, Cindy, my sweet."

They had their picture taken and the engagement was announced in the local papers and also in her home town paper. Invitations were being addressed. This was done at the apartment where the remodeling was coming along with surprising speed.

"Oh, Reg, all of these people—senators, representatives, even the Lieutenant Governor. Surely you don't expect them all to come."

"They are all friends of mine," he assured her.

Uncle Matt and Aunt Kate had insisted on buying Cynthia her gown and paying for the flowers. When she protested, Matt exclaimed, "Please don't deprive us of this privilege, Cindy. We don't have a daughter, and you seem like one to us. So, please . . ."

So she consented, and Kate had gone with her to select her gown. Nothing but the best would do for her. When Cynthia again protested at the cost, Kate said, "Please, dear, we want to do it. We can afford it and I'm having the time of my life. Besides, you are marrying a very popular senator, you know."

"I know, and sometimes it frightens me."

"Well, don't let it," her aunt declared. "You are as good as any of them, my dear."

"You could be prejudiced," Cynthia murmured.

"Well," Kate smiled, "if I am, then let me be."

The foliage season had drawn to a close and the ground lay carpeted with the fallen leaves still reflecting the beauty of the season, so business slackened at the resort. Cynthia had more time for her wedding plans.

Andrea consented to be her maid of honor and Joan her only bridesmaid. Sara would be the flower girl and Nathan Harrison the ring bearer.

"And I'd like Jerry to sing, Reg, if it's okay with you. Gretchen will play the organ, I'm sure."

It was all agreeable to Reg. Greg promised to be his best man and Jeff and Cory would be ushers. Ken would have part of the service with the local pastor.

Cynthia's parents insisted on paying for the reception which would be held in the church vestry and would be catered. Lucy Thomas took Cynthia to a company which was excellent in that capacity. Janelle Phillips offered to make the wedding cake and Cynthia asked her to serve it, as well. A photographer was hired and Alex promised to take a video.

"Have we forgotten anything, Reg?" Cynthia inquired as they were hanging curtains in their living room one evening during the middle of November.

"If we have, it's just too bad. Hey, careful!" he shouted as she dropped the curtain rod on which a snowy white curtain had been placed. His shout made her jump and as she let go, it crumpled in a heap on the carpeted floor.

"Oh, no, and I just spent hours pressing them," she sighed, suddenly bursting into tears.

"Hey, don't cry. It's not a national disaster." Picking her up in his arms he carried her to a deep chair and cradled her in his arms.

Her crying turned to shaky but happy laughter as her arms crept around his neck. "I guess I'm just tired."

"Well, let it all go for now. You just rest for awhile. Besides, this is cozy, isn't it? We really haven't had much leisure time together, have we?" After a few minutes he stated, "Saturday we are going to let everything go and spend the day together just the two of us—or at least the afternoon."

"What will we do? Where can we go? I do wish I had a home nearby where I could entertain you."

"Don't worry. I'll think of something special."

"I know you will, darling," she sighed contentedly. "Reg, let's always love each other as we do right now. Let's not let our marriage grow cold—like some—let's be like the Holloways and Jeff and Sylvia . . ."

"Yes, honey," he agreed softly, fervently.

"You know, my mother has finally agreed to come. They'll drive, leaving on Thanksgiving Day and arriving late Friday afternoon. I think one thing that made her decide to come was Oliver going into the service. She couldn't have faced Thanksgiving Day at home without him."

"What about you?"

"Oh, I'm used to that. I'm really trying—and I believe I've succeeded—at least partially—in having a feeling of genuine affection for her."

"That's good, darling."

"Believe me, if we ever have a daughter—well, I hope I've learned something." Sitting up abruptly, she said, "I hope you know I can't cook very well. I've never had the opportunity to learn."

"You can learn on me, dear. And," he teased, "don't forget we will be living in the same house with my mother. I can always sneak downstairs for a bite if you starve me."

"Reginald Thomas, you wouldn't!" she cried.

"Honey, I'll be so ecstatic with you sitting across the table from me that I probably won't even know what I'm eating."

Snuggling against his shoulder once again, she answered, "I love you, too. But I'll learn—just give me time. Now I'd better get home, it's getting late. I'll have Aunt Kate help me with the curtains tomorrow."

Thanksgiving Day had come and gone. The Holloway home was full of guests. Since Jerry Thorpe was to take part in Cynthia's wedding, Andrea thought it would be a good idea for the Holloways to celebrate the holiday with them. So the Thorpe family and the elder Holloways were there. The Harrison home was also filled with guests.

Cynthia and her uncle and aunt had been invited to the Thomases. Lucy Thomas was indeed graciously welcoming Cynthia's family in a sincere manner.

Cynthia was lovingly ordered by Andrea and Joan Fisher to sleep late on Friday. They would see that the vestry was appropriately decorated for the reception. Janelle Phillips was taking charge of the cake table. Everyone was so kind, Cynthia felt very much loved and wanted.

Her parents arrived around three o'clock. Cynthia was nervous about meeting her mother, and indeed, Maude Marsh was at first critical and sharp-tongued. "What an out-of-the-way place you have chosen to live in, Cynthia. I would be bored to death."

"That's because you don't know the people, Mother."

"I expect with all the wealth they possess according to your father, they are all very uppity."

"You couldn't be more wrong, Mother. Wait until you meet them. Now, let's go see Uncle Matt and Aunt Kate. They are anxious to see you."

"I'll bet," was the slightly sarcastic answer.

When they met Matt, he held out his hand to his sister. "I'm so glad to see you after all these years, Maude."

She touched his hand briefly. "It was inevitable under the circumstances."

Kate welcomed them warmly, then asked Maude if she would like to rest until supper time when they would eat in the resort dining room.

"Don't we have to register?" Norman asked.

"You are our guests," Matt answered. "It's all taken care of."

"In that case, I think I will rest awhile. What time is the rehearsal, Cynthia?" Maude asked.

"Around seven, Mother."

"I suppose it's necessary for me to be there."

"I'd like to have you there."

"All right then, I'll go," she agreed a bit coolly.

The rehearsal was exciting and just a bit chaotic. When Cynthia saw Lucy Thomas exerting herself to put Maude Marsh at ease, and when her mother smiled and entered into the conversation with Lucy and Kate, she relaxed. Ralph and Lucy invited the wedding party and their families to one of Ralph's chicken barbecues after the rehearsal. Cynthia's pleasure mounted as she watched her mother's attitude change.

The wedding was beautiful. Everyone commented on what a radiant bride Cynthia was, in her bridal finery, and how happy the bridegroom appeared. Cynthia was so deliriously happy, feeling secure in Reg's love, that even the attendance of the dignitaries from the State Legislative branch failed to arouse any qualms. After the reception and most of the guests had left, Cynthia, still looking radiant in her brown mink-collared suit, and Reg, handsome in a brown pinstripe suit, caused a flurry of activity as she threw her bouquet, after which they escaped hand in hand midst a shower of rice, to Reg's car which was colorfully decorated with crepe paper and noisy with clanging tin cans.

Lucy invited Norman, Maude, Matt and Kate to their home for a snack because, as she said, "We are all family now and we need someone to talk over the wedding with."

At the Holloway home, the Thorpe family, Greg's parents, Jeff, Sylvia, Lydia, Gramps and Gretchen Nelson were discussing the day's events over a light snack.

"Well," Jason grinned, "you must admit we found a man for Miss Marsh after all."

"What do you mean—we?" Greg raised an eyebrow.

"She met Reg here, didn't she? And I would like to point out that several romances developed at The Farm this year. Even those two," he rolled his eyes in the direction of Jerry and Gretchen who had found a secluded corner where they were holding hands and whispering. "I heard Jerry ask Mom if he could come here for part of his Christmas vacation. He's sure got it bad."

"Don't knock young love, Jason. Look at your Aunt Sylvia and me. Our romance began in our teen years," Jeff reproved him.

"Oh, I know, Uncle Jeff. Your romance is a legend in the Roberts family—still—I hope Cupid keeps his hands off my life until I accomplish some of my goals."

"Such as?" his mother prodded.

"For a start, after high school I want to attend a Christian college where I can major in business administration and take some Bible courses as well."

"Sounds like commendable aspirations," Greg said. "But," he teased, "I noticed you didn't ignore the girls this summer."

"You mean they didn't ignore me," he protested. Then grinning he continued, "Ah, they're all right in their place but deliver me for a few years. And, Nan," he said, turning to his grandmother, "my fondest dream is to see The Farm run exclusively as a Bible Conference—which it is, in a sense, now."

Lydia replied, "I think I'd like that, too, Jason. We'll work on it, shall we? But, Jason, I do hope you're not serious about a career that doesn't include a wife . . ."

"Hey, I never said that—I just think first things first . . ."

"And," Greg teased, "when he finally falls in love, it's my opinion he'll fall hard . . ."

'Well, with this place being the setting for so many romances, I'll be in the right place, won't I? As for now, Becky is my best girl," he added, kissing his small sister on the head as she crawled onto his lap.

"And me, too?" Sara asked anxiously.

Jason chuckled. "And you, too, Sara."

JOYCE HASKELL FROST, a freelance writer, lives in her native Vermont whose beautiful rugged scenery provides picturesque background material for her novels. High on her priority of hobbies is reading.

Joyce, who became a Christian at age 35, was for years active in the local church. She and her husband, Vern, also served several years on staff at Harvey Cedars Bible Conference in Harvey Cedars, New Jersey.

Joyce now delights in sharing her faith through her Christian romances. THE YEARNING HEART, a sequel to BANNER OF LOVE, is her seventh book released under the imprint of WELLSPRING BOOKS which she and her husband publish.

WELLSPRING BOOKS is dedicated to providing readers with enjoyable romantic fiction containing a vibrant Christian witness.